"Kit, Just What Are You Asking Me?"

Summer questioned gently.

Kit shook her head, her eyes revealing her newly awakened love. "I suppose I'm trying to ask you what it feels like when you're in love," she admitted to her friend. "I never have been, you know."

"Tyler?"

Kit nodded. "Black eyes, sexy body, et cetera."

Summer frowned. "This really has you tied up in knots, hasn't it?"

"That's putting it mildly. One minute I'm up and the next I'm down. Emotional roller coasting is not my idea of the way I want to live."

A tiny smile curved Summer's lips. "Well, honey, all I can say is welcome to the human race."

SARA CHANCE

is a "wife, mother, author, in that order," who currently resides in Florida with her husband. With the ocean minutes from her front door, Ms. Chance enjoys both swimming and boating.

Dear Reader:

SILHOUETTE DESIRE is an exciting new line of contemporary romances from Silhouette Books. During the past year, many Silhouette readers have written in telling us what other types of stories they'd like to read from Silhouette, and we've kept these comments and suggestions in mind in developing SILHOUETTE DESIRE.

DESIREs feature all of the elements you like to see in a romance, plus a more sensual, provocative story. So if you want to experience all the excitement, passion and joy of falling in love, then SILHOUETTE DESIRE is for you.

Karen Solem
Editor-in-Chief
Silhouette Books

SARA CHANCE
A Touch of Passion

Silhouette Desire

Published by Silhouette Books New York

America's Publisher of Contemporary Romance

Silhouette Books by Sara Chance

Her Golden Eyes (DES #46)
Home at Last (DES #83)
This Wildfire Magic (DES #107)
A Touch of Passion (DES #183)

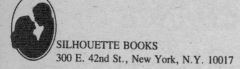

SILHOUETTE BOOKS
300 E. 42nd St., New York, N.Y. 10017

Copyright © 1985 by Sydney Ann Clary
Cover artwork copyright © 1985 Howard Rogers

Distributed by Pocket Books

ISBN: 0-373-05002-X

First Silhouette Books printing January, 1985

10 9 8 7 6 5 4 3 2 1

America's Publisher of Contemporary Romance

Printed in the U.S.A.

BC91

For Robin, my friend, agent and
fellow romance lover

Touch me in passion
Touch me in love
My heart is yours
Your heart is mine
Together we hold forever.

1

━◦◦◦◦◦◦◦◦◦◦━

Good crowd, huh, boss?" Ben murmured as he paused beside the woman leaning casually against the gleaming mahogany bar. He wiped a nonexistent smudge from the highly polished surface of his pride and joy.

Kit Mallory smiled, her unusual sherry-colored eyes lighting with amusement at her cousin's careful attention. Regardless of the kinship between them, Ben was probably the best bartender Mallory's Pub had ever had. "The season's finally starting," Kit replied, her gaze shifting from Ben's open face to the late Friday night crowd filling the lounge to capacity.

Most of the people present were familiar to her. The old couple in the corner had come every Friday for the past eighteen years. The office group over by the band were celebrating the end of another week, while a pair of newlyweds cuddled together on the dance floor to the beat of a slow number. Friends, lovers, marrieds, each was just a representative of the customers who frequented her pub. And Kit knew the majority of them by name. Dan had taught her well before he died. The thought of her generous, blunt-spoken stepfather brought a hint of sadness to her eyes. Even after five years she still missed his friendship and support.

"He would have been proud of your renovations," Ben commented quietly, interrupting Kit's thoughts.

Startled at Ben's perception, Kit glanced back. "How did you know I was thinking of Dan?"

"Were you?" Ben's expression showed his surprise. "You still miss him, don't you?"

Kit nodded. "At moments like this I do. He would have enjoyed all the noise, music and laughter."

She glanced back across the happy throng, her eyes probing the shadowed perimeter tables in an automatic search for a haven in the tastefully elegant new decor of burgundy, cream and silver. Idly, she monitored the progress of her senior waitress as Betty drifted from seating to seating, collecting empty glasses and chatting with customers.

Then out of the darkness a figure moved, disturbing the scene. A head lifted so that the dim light focused on jet black hair as thick as a wild stallion's mane. Lines, planes and hollows formed a bronze face beneath the shaggy forelock highlighting the darkest eyes Kit had ever seen. Eyes that watched her with an unwavering intensity unlike anything she'd ever encountered. Waves of hostility fanned out from his seemingly relaxed body to encircle her.

Shocked by the depth of the emotion directed at her by a man she had never seen before, Kit studied him openly. Black! The color and the word were borne on the breath of a sigh and rose as a definition of the unknown watcher. Black hair, black eyes, black turtle-neck over black denim jeans echoed the dark anger she sensed in him. What had she done to earn his wrath?

"What's she doing here?"

Ben's urgently muttered words abruptly drew Kit's attention to first his worried face and then, in response to his nod, to the entrance of the pub. A petite blonde stood indecisively in the doorway, scanning the room with an almost frantic look.

Ben started around the bar to go to her.

"No, let me." Kit stopped him swiftly with a hand on his arm. "Whatever it is, you don't want her breaking down out here. I'll take her back to the office and see if I can find out what's wrong."

Ben nodded, his eyes never leaving the delicate figure of his distraught girl friend. "Hurry."

Hardly hearing the unnecessary plea, Kit glided agilely between tables, responding with a smile to the friendly calls of her regular patrons, but without wasting a second in reaching Lydia's side. Lydia Nelson had entered their lives more than three months before and, in that time, Kit had handled a number of her emotional scenes. Lydia was a volatile mixture of charm, temper and budding maturity that often gave lie to her nineteen years.

"Kit," the younger woman breathed, her voice catching on what sounded suspiciously like a sob, "I had to come. I had to warn you."

"Warn me?" Kit repeated, subtly guiding the dainty blonde toward the hallway on the opposite side of the room. As always when confronted with Lydia's extravagant words, Kit found herself downplaying the girl's dramatics.

Lydia grabbed her, her nails digging briefly into Kit's arm. "He's coming. God knows, he may already be here. He's going to wring my neck, I just know it."

"Calm down," Kit commanded, inwardly sighing with relief when they entered the shadowy corridor to her private domain. The click of the door shutting behind them was as welcome as the sudden muting of the boisterous gaiety of the lounge. "No one will bother you here and you know it. Between me, Ben and Shadow, you're safe."

"I hope so."

"Let's sit down and you can tell me what's going on." Kit led the way to her office, wondering if Lydia would ever learn to restrain her volatile temperament.

Discipline over her own emotional nature had taken Kit years to achieve. Through painful experience and Dan's gentle guidance, she had learned the value of properly channeled energy. It was this acquired trait that allowed her to function so successfully in her competitive, sometimes questionable and almost totally male-dominated field. Regardless of the circumstances, outwardly she projected a serene image of power and self-assurance. If she had doubts, and she was honest enough to admit she did, she kept them well hidden. Hopefully, one day Lydia too would learn the value of self-discipline.

"Now, suppose you start at the beginning," Kit suggested when they were seated. She leaned back in her chair. One hand dropped to stroke the sleek, wedge-shaped head of the Doberman that had been at her side from the moment she left the lounge's main room. Shadow by name as well as actions, the dog was Kit's constant companion, unobtrusive bodyguard and friend.

"It's Uncle Ty," Lydia began in a rush. "Mom called Jacksonville yesterday to tell him about the problems we've been having. She made it sound like I'm some kind of rebel or something." Lydia jumped to her feet, her eyes flashing. "She treats me like such a child!" She paced restlessly in front of Kit's desk. "She has no right. I'm a woman, not some rebellious kid."

Kit watched Lydia's agitated movements, wondering again at the nineteen-year-old's curious dependency on her parent's approval and her overly dramatic behavior. If she hadn't checked Lydia's ID herself, she'd wonder if the girl had lied about her age. In spite of her decidedly mature appearance, Lydia acted all too often like a girl of sixteen or seventeen.

"Lydia, sit down," Kit ordered calmly, realizing from experience that she must curtail Lydia's theatrical tendencies.

Startled by Kit's tone of authority, Lydia swung around and plopped down onto the chair. "Damn, haven't you heard a word I've said? Uncle Ty will be furious because Mom called him down here to settle this mess," Lydia exclaimed bitterly. "He hates leaving his business and he's going to be mad as fire at you."

"Me?" Kit repeated, momentarily at a loss to make the connection. "Why me?"

"Because I'm not—"

Shadow's deep-throated warning growl cut through Lydia's words only seconds before the door to Kit's office flew open to reveal that man, the unknown watcher in black.

"So your mother was right," Harrison Tyler grated harshly, his eyes flickering contemptuously over the scene. His gaze raked Kit's slender figure before coming to rest on the alert, growling dog at her side. "Call him off," he demanded roughly.

"Why should I?" Kit countered evenly, while every nerve tightened in readiness for the confrontation looming on the horizon. More curious than afraid, Kit waited for his next move. From the corner of her eye, she was aware of the sudden pallor of Lydia's face and her defiant expression.

"Look, lady, call your mutt off. I have no intention of adding dog bites to my list of grievances against you." Without waiting to see if Kit obeyed him, his stormy gaze swung to his belligerent niece. "You may be seventeen, young lady, but your behavior is little better than a fifteen-year-old's. Do you have any idea what you've put your mother through with this little escapade? Do you even care?"

"Of course I care," Lydia shot back, lunging to her feet. "The problem is she doesn't care about me. And neither do you."

"You think not?" he drawled, flicking an insulting

14

look around Kit's office before eyeing Kit herself with deliberation.

Kit met his gaze, wondering if he could see the shock he had dealt her with the disclosure of Lydia's age. Seventeen! The girl was a minor, underage, and she had served her in the lounge. An infraction like that could get her license revoked at the worst and at the very least put a blot on her carefully guarded reputation. Right on the heels of that realization came the knowledge that the liquor licensing board might well be the least of her problems. Harrison Tyler appeared ready to wring someone's neck and Kit didn't need two guesses to figure out whose he had in mind.

"Quiet, Shadow." Kit silenced her canine protector with the softly spoken command in the German he had been trained to obey. "You'd better come in and have a seat," she suggested evenly, her gaze steady on her unexpected visitor. "I believe there are some explanations to be made."

Tyler gave a sharp gesture of assent before stepping forward and closing the door behind him. His ebony eyes held hers as he crossed the wide expanse of carpet to take a chair directly across the desk from her.

His eyes narrowed as Kit showed neither discomfort nor surprise at his challenging inspection. Baffled and reluctantly intrigued by the impenetrable cloak of tranquillity emanating from her, he felt some of his anger over the problem of Lydia dissolve. Curiosity about the woman before him made him restrain his temper in an effort to see what she would do next. Giving in to his interest he studied her closely.

Hair the shade of rich chestnut lay in a heavy plait across one shoulder so that the feathery ends caressed the soft swell of her breast with every breath she took. Brown eyes the color of Amaretto stared calmly into his, reflecting a self-possession far beyond anything he'd ever experienced. There was no beauty in the cleanly sculpted lines of her face, yet neither was this strange woman plain. Rather, she was like a placid mountain lake, cool, clear and untouched by the pollution of mankind. Surprised by his fanciful train of thought, Tyler searched for outward signs of the disreputable life she led. After all, the woman was the owner of one of the most popular night spots on this part of Florida's Gold Coast. She couldn't be as unaffected by her occupation as she appeared.

While her opponent was sizing her up, Kit did a little visual investigating of her own. In her business she met all kinds of people, but she couldn't remember one who had the impact on her that this man did. Even in the dimly lit lounge he had sprung vividly alive from the shadows. But now, in the brighter light of her sanctum, his power and presence were magnified. Lean and obviously fit in spite of his desk-bound position as owner of Tyler Advertising, he topped six feet by two inches or a shade more. Yet his features, rather than his physical stature, held her attention. Midnight eyes beneath straight black brows dominated the experience-lined face. Harrison Tyler, self-made success story and Florida's PR genius, lounged in her comfortably overstuffed chair with all the bold assurance of a man who knew his own power.

"Satisfied?" he drawled when Kit lifted her gaze to his.

"Are you?" she returned, employing the same sardonic emphasis he had. Neither of them paid the slightest attention to Lydia's irritated flounce.

"Well, isn't this just great. You two can play staring games some other time, if you don't mind," Lydia exclaimed. She dropped into her chair, a frown marring the curve of her lips. Cornflower blue eyes holding a mixture of hurt and youthful defiance focused on Kit. "Why didn't you make him leave?"

Kit sensed the anxiety and the lost child's need for reassurance beneath Lydia's antagonistic pose. She shook her head gently, her gaze compassionate. Whatever lies Lydia had told and however many problems her deception had or would cause them all, she was troubled and she needed help. Now more than ever.

"What good would it have done, Lydia? If what he says is true, he had a right to come after you," Kit answered quietly.

"He's not my father. He's only—"

"Lydia." Kit silenced her outburst. She knew Lydia's continued emotionalism was only aggravating an already complicated situation. At the moment Harrison Tyler was controlling his anger well, but being goaded by his niece was guaranteed to strain his resources.

"I'll say one thing for you, you train people and dogs very well," Tyler murmured, making no effort to disguise the mockery in his voice. He glanced first at his indignantly gasping relative, then at the obedient Doberman eyeing him so alertly.

Kit acknowledged the dubious compliment but deliberately ignored his offensive tone. Until she understood him better she had no intention of confronting Tyler over his mistaken impression. Thanks to Lydia, she knew a great deal about him and his sister, Emily, Lydia's mother.

"Am I correct in assuming Lydia's mother sent for you to rescue Lydia from her association with me?"

One dark brow slanted upward at the obvious nature of her question. "You are," he answered shortly.

"And both of you believe I knew Lydia to be a minor and therefore underage to be in a bar or to be served liquor?"

He nodded, his eyes gleaming with curiosity in spite of the banked anger still smoldering in their onyx depths.

Kit turned, pinning Lydia with a shrewd look, holding out her hand, palm up. "Your handbag."

Lydia grasped the crocheted square tightly for a moment before finally releasing it. "I'm sorry," Lydia whispered, unable to withstand the disappointment she saw reflected in her friend and confidante's expression.

"I know," Kit soothed her, well able to understand how Lydia had succumbed to the temptation of lying in the first place. She upended the purse, spilling the contents in a small heap on the mirrorlike surface of her desk. Two slender fingers sifted through the pile to extract a well-worn wallet. A second later she extended two different driver's licenses to the man watching her every move intently.

"Until tonight I had no idea how old Lydia really was," she explained flatly. "I've spent too many years of my life—not to mention quite a bit of money—on this place to jeopardize it or my reputation over something like serving a known minor."

Tyler stared down at the damning IDs he held, then back at Kit's composed face. "I should have thought a woman with your experience would have been suspicious of a girl this young even if she did have the proper identification."

Kit's eyebrows lifted at the innuendo contained in his words. She wondered briefly how such an attractively husky voice could convey such a jagged edge of sarcasm.

"Unfortunately in this case, my experience, as you call it, did not equip me to read Lydia's mind about her birthday," she replied, mimicking Ty's tone but without the heat he'd used.

"Well, at least my sister can rest easy about Lydia coming back here now that you know the truth," Ty stated, his eyes challenging her to disagree.

"Uncle Ty, you can't mean that," Lydia gasped. "Tell him, Kit, please," she pleaded, without giving him a chance to answer her. "I won't cause any trouble. I need you and Ben."

Feeling torn in two directions, Kit hesitated fractionally. On the one hand, Harrison Tyler had a legal right to demand that Lydia stay out of Mallory's, yet on the other, Lydia really did seem to need the emotional support she got from her and Ben.

"Who's Ben?" Ty questioned sharply, studying Lydia suspiciously.

Lydia glanced frantically at Kit, panic in her eyes. "Kit's cousin," she stammered.

Tyler's midnight-maned head swung around to pin Kit with an accusing glare. "Just how old is this cousin?"

"Twenty-two."

"Good God," he swore, his expression rapidly losing its controlled mask.

"It's not what you think." Lydia rushed into disjointed speech. "He's a friend. I can talk to him—to Kit. You haven't been here. You don't know what it's been like since Dad walked out on Mom and me. She's working all the time. When I need her she's too tired or else she's gone. My friends pity me. The boys think because Dad fooled around, I should too—"

There was a visible though slight softening in Ty as he listened to Lydia's halting explanation. "Okay, Lydia," he interrupted, holding up one well-kept hand. Tension drained from his body, easing some of the weariness of a long week, the worry over Emily's desperate phone call, the traveling at a second's notice and the emotional scene he had been catapulted into. Tiredly, he raked his fingers through his hair in a bachelor's frustration over how to deal with a rebellious teenager.

"Look, honey, you can't keep coming here. This is no place for you," he began reasonably.

Kit sat back, unobtrusively withdrawing from the scene. Watching the careful way he was trying to avoid upsetting Lydia in spite of his own temper, Kit found herself feeling surprisingly sympathetic toward him.

"I can if I want to," Lydia shot back, pale but still defiant. "As long as I don't drink I'm not breaking any laws. And Kit won't throw me out, will you?"

Finding herself impaled by two sets of eyes, one pair pleading and the other demanding, Kit knew she had to make a choice. "Your uncle's right," she murmured gently, wishing she didn't need to hurt the girl by a seeming rejection. "You shouldn't be here, but that doesn't mean you can't stop by my town house when you want to talk. Or call me here or at home."

"You're not turning me out?" Lydia's voice rose in a squeak of disbelief mingled with distress.

Kit opened her lips to reassure her when Ty intervened. "You're not being fair, Lydia. Ms. Mallory is only showing good sense. She has a business to run here, not a hangout for underage kids. This is no place for you and she knows it, even if you don't," he said firmly, but with a note of compassion in his deep voice.

Gently spoken though it was, Kit was stunned at Ty's summation. How dare he speak for her? Who did he think he was to pretend to know what she thought? She'd taken a lot from this man, but this was beyond anything. It had been years since anyone had helped her make her decisions. Her temper rose.

"I hate you," Lydia cried, jumping to her feet. "You're making her do this to me. I was happy here and Mom couldn't stand it, so she sent for you to ruin it for me."

Lydia's almost hysterical denunciation stopped Kit before she could give way to her own feelings. In a split second her justifiable anger died as she recognized the knife-edge control Lydia still retained.

"That's not true, honey," Tyler sought to soothe her as one would a child. "Your mother and I only want what's good for you."

"Good?" Lydia repeated in a shrill wail. "I'm sick of good . . ." She turned to Kit. "I need you. This is where I want to be. Tell him you'll let me stay."

"I can't." Kit spoke the damning words, hating every syllable. "You can come to me anywhere but here." She turned her head, her gaze focusing on Ty's set face. Lydia too glared at her uncle, her whole body tensed, poised for flight.

Tyler stared at the two women confronting him. Damn Kit Mallory for her interference and damn Lydia's youthful vulnerability, he swore in silent frustration. He wanted nothing more than to take Lydia away from this place. But he couldn't. That female had seen to that. And there she sat like some statue, seemingly unmoved by the emotions driving both Lydia and himself. For a moment he'd actually thought he had pierced the cloak of aloofness that surrounded her and had felt a surge of satisfaction at her signs of temper. But in a fraction of a heartbeat the tiny betrayal had been subdued by her apparent concern for his niece.

Irritated beyond measure by her inexplicable concern, Ty returned his attention to Lydia. He acknowledged with a sigh that there was only one course open to him, distasteful though he found it. "All right, I won't try to keep you from seeing Ms. Mallory on the condition you stay away from the bar." He eyed her sternly before pinning Kit with a dark look. "But both of you understand this. If I catch Lydia here or learn that she's been here, I'll report you to the liquor licensing board. Is that clear?"

"Very," Kit agreed drily, with no doubt he meant every word.

"What's a liquor board?" Lydia demanded, recognizing the threat without understanding it.

"Do I explain or do you?" Kit asked, her brows lifting slightly to emphasize her sardonic question.

Tyler nodded silently, wondering again how this woman could remain so untouched. Her control was phenomenal. Save for the faintest sting in the slow, melodic cadence of her speech, she seemed totally unmoved by anything except her concern for Lydia.

"The liquor licensing board is responsible for issuing my permit to operate a pub. It's also responsible for seeing to it that I adhere to the governing policies and rules of the state. In the event of a violation, such as serving a minor, I could have my license revoked or suspended, or be hit with a stiff fine. Either way, it's not good," Kit concluded bluntly.

"You mean I could be the cause of Mallory's being closed?" Lydia asked worriedly, momentarily diverted from her problems by this new development.

"It could happen—"

"It will happen," Ty corrected swiftly.

In a flash Lydia's anxiety for Kit died beneath her

glare of open insurrection. "Don't worry, Uncle. I won't come here again," she vowed, rushing for the door before either of the adults guessed her intention.

"Damn," Tyler swore as he bolted after her.

Kit, with Shadow at her side, was right on his heels as he catapulted into the corridor. They were just in time to see the back door leading to the alley slam shut.

"She'll be making for the front parking lot. Shadow and I will follow her to be sure she gets there all right. If you go through the lounge, you'll be there ahead of her. The last thing we need is for her to try driving in the mood she's in."

Ty raked her with furious eyes. "If you had stayed out of this in the beginning, we wouldn't be in this mess now," he bit out between clenched teeth.

Kit was already moving away as he spoke. At his angry words, she hesitated just long enough to deliver her own observation. "If Lydia had someone at home to listen to her, she wouldn't have chosen a bar for companionship and forgetfulness." Ignoring his sharp intake of breath, she spun on her heel and raced for the door. She had wasted precious seconds while Lydia was running through a darkened—hopefully deserted—alleyway. With a soft German command to Shadow to seek, she opened the door on the small pool of light surrounded by the darkness of a moonless night. Lydia was nowhere to be seen.

"Which way?" she demanded of the dog.

Shadow woofed once in response before gliding into the inky velvet to the right. Kit followed swiftly, secure in his guidance. Together, they raced down the long, narrow asphalt path that eventually led back to the street parking lot.

"There she is," she murmured half to herself as she caught sight of a flicker of movement ahead. Slowing her pace so she would remain undetected, Kit rounded the corner and stopped at the edge of the darkened attorney's office that was her nearest neighbor.

Before her spread a well-lit sea of vehicles of assorted shapes and sizes. Lydia was weaving her way toward her own set of wheels through this obstacle course. From her vantage point, Kit followed Lydia's progress as she came ever closer to the motionless form of her uncle, who stood beside her car. She watched as the girl slid to a surprised halt before backing away, her head shaking vehemently from side to side. The raised sounds of her angry refusals and Ty's deeper responses carried clearly on the night air although Kit was unable to distinguish their exact words. Seconds ticked by as the man and the girl faced each other; then Lydia flung herself at her uncle and buried her face in his shoulder.

Strong arms gathered her slender figure against his strength, his fingers threading through the silky strands of blond hair in a calming gesture.

"Good," Kit breathed, releasing a relieved sigh. For a moment she'd been afraid Tyler wouldn't offer Lydia the sympathy she needed. And, oddly, she had known a deep sense of disappointment at the possibility. Shaking her head at the unexpected importance she'd placed on Ty's reaction, she stared across the crowded lot and found her gaze locking with his. Although she was unable to read the expression in those black eyes, she felt the power of his ebony stare. His frustration with the current situation and his anger at her involvement with Lydia were all telegraphed in a sizzling message on the soft balmy breeze. Yet he obviously loved his niece.

It was the realization of that love that held Kit motionless as a flood of memories of another time when a strong man and a troubled teen had faced each other in a situation so very similar to this one washed over her. Only then it had been Dan, her soon-to-be stepfather, reasoning with an angry fifteen-year-old Kit.

How self-righteously angry she had been. She'd been so full of her own hurt at having been brought up by her overworked waitress mother. Like Lydia, she had thought only of herself and her needs until Dan made her really look at herself. With the advent of the gruff, kind-hearted man into her life, she had begun the slow struggle to maturity. Now it was Lydia's turn. And because of Dan and the debt she owed him for his care and the generosity he'd shown her, Kit had wanted to help Lydia the same way. It was for Lydia's sake she'd held her temper even when she'd been sorely tried.

The memory of Ty's far from subtle remarks drew her out of the past to refocus her attention on the scene before her. She sighed silently, wishing she could reassure Tyler of her very real desire to help his niece. But she couldn't, at least not now; he'd seen what she did for a living and judged her accordingly.

Saddened, without really understanding why it should mean so much to her, Kit turned away to glide soundlessly through the shadows back to her own world.

2

~**∘∘∘∘∘∘∘∘∘∘∘**~

Kit reentered the pub and made her way down the corridor to the main lounge. It was near closing and time for her walk-through, a practice begun shortly after she took over the tavern. At first, she'd been extremely young—only twenty-three—and a female to boot, so she hadn't spent the evenings holding court at one end of the long mahogany bar as Dan had done. Instead, she had kept a low profile, being on hand personally for only a half hour on opening and another thirty minutes at the end of each evening. During these short appearances, she'd greeted regular customers, met new ones and in general helped promote the friendly neighborhood atmosphere for which Mallory's was known.

Making a conscious effort to put the scene between

Tyler and Lydia from her mind, Kit began her passage between tables. With a smile here, a word there, she cast a knowledgeable eye over the slowly emptying room, noting those who were lingering and those already saying their good-byes.

"Nice crowd," she commented to Ben on reaching the bar.

Ben nodded. A slight grin for the benefit of the patrons lining the long counter curved his mouth without reaching his hazel eyes. "The band's been good, too," he added above the noise of the music and conversation. With seeming nonchalance, he collected various empty glasses until he'd worked his way close enough to Kit to permit a private word.

"Everything okay?"

Kit hitched a knee over the burgundy-padded bar stool, positioning herself so that her body screened them temporarily from the rest of the room. "Lydia's fine," she hastened to assure him. "But we need to talk."

Puzzled by the tone of her voice, Ben's brow wrinkled in a frown. "I'll be finished in about forty-five minutes," he told her as a man at the other end of the bar held his glass aloft in the age-old call for a refill. Ben suppressed a grimace before stepping away. "See you later."

With a smile to the couple sitting beside her, Kit slipped off her perch to return to her office and the paperwork awaiting her attention. She was just finishing up the tedious task when Ben, cash drawer in hand, appeared in her doorway.

"Finally," he sighed wearily as he laid the metal tray in front of Kit. "What a week!" He flopped limply into the chair that Harrison Tyler had occupied earlier. The contrast between the two men couldn't have been more vivid. Both were lean and fit, yet there was an intrinsic toughness in Tyler that was lacking in the younger Ben. Where Tyler's concern for Lydia had been mixed with anger and frustration, Ben's anxiety was clearly evident in spite of his tiredness. Where Tyler had worn his day's exhaustion with an air of undiminished vitality, Ben appeared weighed down, finely drawn and older than his years. Yet Kit knew there was strength and kindness in her cousin that a girl like Lydia would find appealing.

"How's Lydia?" he asked worriedly. He glanced around as though looking for her.

"She's fine," Kit replied, wishing there was some way to soften her next words. "Ben, Lydia lied to us. She's seventeen, not nineteen."

"What?" he said, sitting upright with a jerk. "She can't be. You checked her ID and so did I." His hazel eyes reflected disbelief as he stared at her. Comprehension dawned slowly, bringing pain and a bleakness Kit hadn't seen in him since he had been discharged from his tour of duty in the Middle East. He had been just Lydia's age when he'd enlisted, but had come back a man four years later.

"It was a fake."

"How did you find out?"

Kit looked down at her hands, lying relaxed on the desk top. She had to be careful what she said now. Ben was no fool, nor was he a coward. He wouldn't hesitate to explain his involvement with Lydia if he felt it was the right thing to do.

"Her uncle, Harrison Tyler, told me. He drove in from Jacksonville tonight after Lydia's mother put in a distress call about us." She raised her eyes to capture his. "From their point of view, we're messin' around with a minor."

"Damn," Ben groaned, slumping back in his seat. "And I probably look like the worse type of cradle-robber."

Kit shook her head, her serious expression emphasizing the compassion in her gaze. "Apparently she hasn't told them about you, at least not in the sense we're talking about."

There was a moment of stunned silence while Ben assimilated this latest shock. "And you didn't explain either?"

"No."

"Why not?"

"For one thing, I don't know exactly what is going on between you two," she pointed out drily. "Other than the fact that you've been seeing each other, neither of you has said much."

"I love her," he stated quietly but with a depth of feeling Kit had never heard from him before. "I want to marry her, but situated as I am, it'll be another year before I can support a wife. And now . . ." his voice trailed off as the full implication of Lydia's deceit hit him. "An underage teenager! It's hard to believe." He grimaced in self-disgust.

"Would you still want to marry her, knowing how young she is?" Kit asked.

Ben glanced up at her careful words. "Of course," he replied immediately, with unshakable conviction. "But you know how I'm set financially. This is my last year on my government educational allowance and I've got one more year to go to my business administration degree. As good a salary as you pay me for part-time bartending, I couldn't support Lydia and pay the rent and my school expenses on what I make."

Kit picked up a pen and idly twirled it between her fingers. "I could help you if you'd let me," she offered, studying her nimble manipulations of the slender instrument.

"No way. It was my decision to enlist after high school. I don't regret those four years. They gave me the direction I needed." He shrugged awkwardly. "Besides, what difference does it make now? Lydia's family isn't likely to consent to our marriage anyway. There's going to be enough of an explosion when I go to them and tell them how we feel."

"I wouldn't do that right now," Kit advised slowly. "Lydia's got enough on her plate as it is. Give things a chance to settle a little. Give her uncle an opportunity to calm her mother down if he can." Or if he wants to, Kit added silently, recalling his condemnation of her and her business.

Ben's curiosity and doubt were evident. "You mean he's more reasonable than Lydia's mother?" he countered skeptically.

"We don't know for sure that Emily Nelson is as unbending as Lydia claims," Kit replied evasively.

"Given half a chance, she might be more understanding than we think. It's evident she cared enough about Lydia to call in her brother to help."

"Or to lend some support," Ben parried, obviously turning her words over in his mind.

"There's that," Kit agreed. "But it won't wash. We were within the law. We checked her identification when we questioned her age and nobody looking at Lydia would guess how young she is. So, as far as the liquor licensing people are concerned, we're covered."

Ben's eyes narrowed thoughtfully. "I get the feeling that's a good thing. Did Lydia's uncle threaten us?"

"No, but I believe he's capable of almost anything to protect his family," she murmured, speaking more from her intuition than from knowledge gained secondhand from Lydia. "He's in a no-win situation at the moment. Plus he's got the added handicap of inexperience as a parent to contend with. He must know he could push Lydia into making a total break with her family if he's not careful. I think he'll try reaching her first before he takes action against us."

Ben nodded. "I still think I should explain about Lydia and me. What if he finds out some other way? It's going to look much worse than it is," Ben said irritably. "If I didn't love Lydia so much, I'd be really angry at her for lying."

Kit tried without success to suppress a chuckle of amusement at Ben's vehemence. "You mean you aren't angry now?" Kit questioned humorously.

"Well, sort of," he grumbled, his mouth curving

into a reluctant grin. "Although how we can see anything funny about this, I don't know."

"A wise man once told me if you can laugh at your problems, you can survive them," Kit quoted softly, remembering her stepfather's favorite philosophy.

"Dan was one smart man," Ben murmured. He rose and stared down at her, all levity wiped from his face. "For Lydia's sake, I'll keep quiet for a while," he declared, returning abruptly to the matter at hand. "I didn't fall in love with Lydia's age. I fell in love with her."

"Okay," Kit agreed, getting to her feet. "I'll back you any way I can. It won't be easy." Her warning was clear, as was her offer of unstinting support. Ben was all that was left of her family and she cared about his happiness as well as Lydia's.

"Thanks, Kit." Ben reached out to touch her cheek in a grateful gesture. "I don't know where this will end, but having you on our side feels good. You're one special lady."

Kit's sherry eyes softened to rich liquid amber and a gentle smile touched her lips. The rare depth of emotion on her usually serene features drew an expression of surprise from Ben.

"The feeling's mutual." She grinned, deliberately lightening the atmosphere. "Now go home and get some rest so I can close the place."

Ben frowned, momentarily diverted from his own worries to comment once more on Kit's—to his mind—disturbing disregard for her own safety. "I wish you wouldn't rely on Shadow so much. I worry about you here alone after we've all gone. I know he's K-9 trained but—" He glanced at the alert animal that was never far from Kit's side.

"I swear you watch over me like a mother hen with only one chick. Shadow's better than a bodyguard and you know it. Nobody bothers a big, snarling dog with a mouthful of sharp, white teeth. And I'm not exactly helpless either," Kit assured him matter-of-factly.

They had had this discussion so often in the past, Kit could almost quote the dialogue by heart. Young though Ben was, he still felt honor bound to watch over her. While she appreciated the affectionate concern behind his protective attitude, she was amused by it, too. Thanks to Dan's insistence, she was well versed in the ways of self-protection, besides being possessed of a tautly trim and physically fit five-foot ten-inch body. With Shadow at her side, Kit felt secure in her solitary life-style, in spite of her odd hours and unusual occupation. Independent by nature, she liked her freedom and made no effort to hide that fact.

"I get the message," Ben conceded ruefully. He raked his hand awkwardly through his light brown hair. "Sometimes I wish you weren't so self-sufficient. It's positively unnerving." He cocked his head to one side, his eyes alight with speculative curiosity. "Don't you ever feel the need to lean on someone? Even as close as you and Dan were, you were still very independent."

Startled by Ben's probing, Kit had no immediate answer. How could she explain the deep well of assurance she felt within herself without sounding impossibly arrogant? It wasn't that she didn't want to share her life with others; it was simply that she had no need to. She was happy as she was, doing what she did, living each day as she chose. She had no one but Ben and Shadow, yet she was content.

"I'm happy, Ben. Surely that's all any of us really want," she replied finally, simply.

"What about love? Don't you want someone to love in your life?" he pressed, suddenly driven to reach her somehow.

"Perhaps one day," she agreed, a faint furrow of uneasiness marring her brow. Oddly, she wasn't really sure if she did want someone to love. She had the feeling that if she found such a man, her life as she now knew and lived it would change.

"Ben, go home," she commanded with mock anger. She was tiring of his questions, yet she didn't want to hurt him by telling him so.

"I'm going," he said, obviously realizing he had said enough.

Kit watched him head for the door, more affected by his words than she wanted to admit. Maybe it was the result of the strange, emotion-packed evening and the abrupt entry of Harrison Tyler into her life.

Inexplicably, her mind filled with the image of Lydia's tear-damp face pressed against his strong shoulder. Not since Dan had Kit known the comfort of having someone to listen to her problems, her fears, her hopes. Dan had been more than a replacement for the father who had deserted her mother before Kit was born. He had been her friend and her mentor, entering her life when she had desperately needed a strong male influence. With his coming, she had learned to control her volatile nature, and to utilize its tremendous energy for achievement instead of rebellion. Through him, she had cultivated tolerance and acceptance; but most of all, she had found a role model of personal integrity whom she still valued and tried to emulate.

Dan was human enough to have faults, yet strong enough to admit his shortcomings and forgive others theirs. He was a unique person, with whom Kit found herself unconsciously comparing the few men in her life. So far she had found no one who came close to him and she knew she needed the strength of character of someone like Dan to match her own strong personality.

Shaking her head to clear it of these introspective thoughts, Kit completed her rounds of the empty bar and let herself out of the front door. After she'd keyed the burglar alarm and locked up, she walked the few steps to reach her new silver Cougar. The presence of a light blue car with Duval County plates parked five spaces away was an annoying reminder of her irate visitor. She frowned briefly, realizing the police would have the vehicle towed away by morning if it remained there.

"Blast that man," she muttered, eyeing the inoffensive sedan irritably. She could call Lydia's to warn him, she supposed. Or better yet, she could call the police to explain the circumstances, she decided on further thought. No sooner had the idea occurred than she was moving toward the phone booth at the edge of the lot.

Beside her Shadow whined his confusion at the change in their normal pattern. Automatically, Kit stroked the dark head to reassure him. "It's okay," she murmured soothingly. It only took a minute to dial the station and explain the situation.

Feeling relieved, Kit slipped into her Cougar with one last glance at the LTD across the way. Suddenly it struck her that she hadn't even considered letting Tyler find his wheels impounded. That thought annoyed her more than any other.

"Damn that man," she swore softly. She started the car with an impatient flick of her wrist and guided it quickly past the Ford onto the street. Concentrating purposefully on the drive home, she crowded Harrison Tyler's persistent image from her mind. She would not let him and his disapproval of her life intrude on her thought any longer.

Her gaze focused on the velvety darkness, broken by the muted orange glow of the interstate lights. The broad highway undulated gently over the streets crisscrossing the flat land surrounding it. Night-shrouded condominiums rose like silent sentinels above the landscape. They were mute testimony of the building boom that had made Palm Beach County one of the fastest growing areas of Florida and the whole country. It was a swiftly changing area she lived in, but she loved it. The year-round good weather, the turquoise Atlantic Ocean only minutes away from almost anywhere and the lush subtropical setting created a rich atmosphere sought by many. The Gold Coast drew tourists from all over the world and Kit made her home right in the center of it all.

Sighing gently as her body relaxed completely, Kit wriggled deeper into the plush bucket seat. Silence broken only by Shadow's faintly audible breathing wrapped her in a peaceful cocoon. Finally she felt restored to her usual calmness. Flicking on her turn signal, she took the exit ramp heading west.

"Almost home, my friend," she murmured when Shadow whined, recognizing their route.

A moment later the Cougar purred quietly through the beautifully landscaped garden entrance of her housing complex. Multicolored spotlights lent an enchanting fairy-tale aura to the slender, feathery palms and assorted plants, while the soft breeze carried the sweetly mingled scents of night-blooming flowers. Kit's town house apartment was situated at the end of a cul-de-sac on a quiet back avenue.

Slipping out of the car, Kit paused for a moment to inhale the fragrance surrounding her. How exquisitely still everything was. This was her favorite time. Peace lay like a benediction over the land. There were no loud noises or raised voices—only the balmy feel of the night against her skin, the brilliant stars glittering across the heavenly canvas overhead and the haven of her home waiting for her just up the path.

Kit let herself into her apartment, ignoring the light switch as she padded soundlessly to her bedroom. Still bathed in the aura of tranquility, she undressed and showered before sliding into her warm, satin-sheeted water bed. Refreshed and relaxed, she stretched lanquidly, then closed her eyes.

She awoke late the next morning to the melodic serenade of a pair of cardinals in the trees outside her patio. She smiled at the sound as she tumbled out of bed and onto the rich royal blue carpet of her bedroom. Shadow greeted her with an exuberant bark as he tossed his tug-rag in her lap in preparation for their morning playtime. Laughing aloud at the canine grin on his intelligent face, Kit made a swift grab for his eagerly quivering body and missed.

"That's cheating," she gasped as he retreated just out of reach. Shadow barked and danced around like an overgrown puppy.

"Okay, okay, I get the message. You want to run in the park. Just let me get some clothes on." Rising in one lithe movement, Kit went to the captain's chest to collect her running shorts and top. She was ready a moment later. After a quick stop in the kitchen to plug in the coffeepot, she and Shadow went out the sliding glass doors, across the patio and through the trees encircling it. Once past the privacy hedge, they entered a lightly wooded area that the tenants fondly called the park. A small man-made lake provided the focal point for several jogging and biking trails, a tennis court and a miniature fleet of paddle boats.

Kit, with Shadow right at her heels, began her run on the short lake path. She nodded pleasantly to a few fellow late-starters as she slowly increased her tempo for the brisk workout so necessary for keeping in shape. She was perspiring freely yet feeling exhilarated from her exercise when she returned home.

A shower and a change of clothes were next on her agenda before she tackled breakfast. She had just finished the latter when the phone rang.

"Summer, what are you doing here?" she demanded on hearing the soft drawl of her caller. "You and Brandon weren't due back for another week."

Summer laughed gaily. "I know, but Brandon decided it was too wet in Boston, so we came back early," she explained.

Kit smiled, trying to imagine the aloof, self-sufficient Brandon Marshall ever being worried about anything as trivial as the weather. "Don't you ever get tired of telling those fibs?" Kit taunted teasingly. "I don't know how Brand puts up with you."

"I'll never tell," Summer returned solemnly, before spoiling the effect by breaking into giggles like a schoolgirl, instead of the thirty-one-year-old married woman she was.

The sound was infectious and Kit found herself enmeshed in her friend's amusement. "So when do I get to see my godchild?" she asked when she finally caught her breath.

"How about tomorrow?" Summer replied promptly. "A barbecue, say about eleven?"

"Okay. Can I bring anything?"

"Nope, just yourself and a man if there is one," Summer returned, a faintly probing note in her husky voice.

Kit's lips lifted in a rueful grimace. Since meeting

Summer shortly after Summer's marriage to Brandon, she'd been drawn more and more to the woman. She was one of the most feminine creatures Kit had ever met, yet Summer had been widowed early and left with a child and a charter fishing business to run in a small town north of West Palm Beach. She had succeeded in running her business and her life while still remaining all woman. Kit admired her for it and for capturing the interest and love of the wealthy and nomadic man who had been one of Dan's best friends.

"Hey, are you still there?" Summer questioned, jarring Kit out of her reverie.

"I'm here. I was just trying to decide which of my many escorts I should call," she quipped.

"I did it again, didn't I?" Summer groaned. "Brandon is going to wring my neck one of these days if I don't learn to control my tongue."

"And your matchmaking," Kit added drily, remembering Summer's last attempt to interest her in a very personable male.

Summer sighed dramatically, drawing a reluctant smile to Kit's lips. "If I promise I won't try to introduce you to any more men, will I be forgiven?"

Kit tipped her head, considering. Summer was amazingly tenacious besides being extremely adept at handling most situations. Somehow her easy assurances were anything but reassuring. "Were you this gung ho on marriage before you caught Brandon?" she demanded curiously.

"No way," Summer denied immediately. "And I'm not now, no matter what you and Brandon say. It's just that when I care about people, I want to see them happy—"

"I'm perfectly content," Kit shot back, feeling suddenly goaded without really knowing why.

"Content is not happy," Summer disagreed gently. "I know, I've been there."

Faced with the realization that Summer very likely really did understand, Kit had no rebuttal. Yes, she had a career and a business she loved, even a home and financial security. But what about her emotional needs? Was she being less than honest in her certainty that she was sufficient unto herself?

"I'll see you at eleven," Kit murmured in farewell. She replaced the receiver and then stared pensively at the rich decor of the home she had created as a retreat.

The colors of sapphire, ruby, ivory and gold abounded in the framework of rough, buff stucco walls and champagne linen drapes. A royal blue carpet stretched through the entire apartment to showcase the crimson accents and dark distressed wood furnishings. Gleaming brass and crystal fixtures reflected tiny prisms of light in the wall of gold-veined mirrors lining one side of the living room. There was life in every vibrant shade in her private sanctum, yet only she and Shadow lived there.

For the first time, Kit wondered if her solitary existence was right for her, or even enough? Surely the roomy captain's chair beside the sofa was more suited to a man's heavier frame than it was to hers. And her king-size water bed? Weren't satin sheets wasted in her almost nunlike life? And those thick burgundy bath sheets that wrapped around her slender curves twice? Everywhere she looked, she saw things that pleased her eye and her love of texture and color, yet not once had she allowed a man to share her domain with her.

Why? There was the question. But where lay the answer?

3

The LTD was gone. Kit gave a satisfied smile at its absence as she parked her car in front of Mallory's and got out. After Summer's unsettling call, she was in no mood for another scene with Harrison Tyler. All she wanted was a nice, normal, boisterous Saturday night with all the usual little problems associated with the weekend crowd.

And that's just what she got when closing time approached without an appearance by Lydia or her ill-tempered uncle. Kit breathed a soft sigh of relief as she strolled down the corridor toward the lounge area. The live band, playing a throbbing rock number, rose above the clink of glasses and conversation, and Kit mentally winced at the noise level.

She threaded her way between tables, tossing a

greeting or smile to those patrons she knew or those who called to her. She froze in her tracks when an arm snaked out to encircle her waist. Her eyes flashed golden sparks of annoyance as she turned to reprimand her captor. The innocently smiling elderly face completely demolished her irritation.

"Pops, you know better than that," she chided humorously, gently detaching the thin arm from around her. She smiled at his two grinning companions. "What are you three doing here on a Saturday? This isn't your bowling night."

All three men chuckled uproariously. Kit's brows raised curiously as she scanned the trio of almost-empty beer glasses on the table. It couldn't be their first round and that was odd for a group that usually confined its imbibing to one drink each.

"Celebrating?" she queried casually.

"You betcha. My granddaughter just had her first baby. I'm a great-granddad now," Pops proclaimed proudly.

"Congratulations," Kit exclaimed in unaffected pleasure, stooping to plant a kiss on his wrinkled cheek. "May I contribute to your party by calling you boys a cab when your're ready to leave? Newly made great-grands deserve a ride home in style."

"Aw, Kit, we aren't that bombed," Pops replied, a twinkle in his eyes.

"Haven't you figured it out, guys? It's my mercenary side showing," she teased in a conspiratorial whisper. "This way you won't stop celebrating so soon."

The three men laughed delightedly at her remark. "Now that's an offer we can't refuse," Pops agreed, his two cronies nodding their gray heads.

"You just tell Betty, your waitress, a few minutes before you're ready to leave and she'll call for me."

Smiling at their undisguised enthusiasm for her offer, Kit headed for the bar, where Betty was talking to Ben.

"Sure, boss, I'll take care of it," the older woman agreed cheerfully when Kit explained the situation.

"I swear, Kit, you've got to be the softest touch around," Ben observed half seriously. "That's the third time this week you've had one of us call for transport."

Surprised at Ben's comment, Kit stared at him blankly for a moment. He knew very well it was the policy of the house to offer any overindulgent patron the same service. Mallory's rarely picked up the tab except in special cases like Pops'.

"What's wrong, Ben?" she asked slowly, seeing the worry beneath his public congeniality. "Is it Lydia?"

He nodded, his gaze making a practiced sweep of the customers seated along the bar. "I haven't heard from her since last night. I felt sure she'd call," he admitted anxiously.

"Take it easy," Kit soothed. "Lydia can't be in any trouble or we would have heard, either from her or her relatives. She's got a lot of explaining to do, don't forget. It's bound to be rough on her right now, so don't add to her problems by going off the deep end. She needs you to be here for her."

"I know," he murmured glumly. "I just wish I knew what was going on."

"So do I." Kit's heartfelt comment brought a quick questioning glance from Ben.

"Trouble?" he asked, catching the disturbed note in her usually calm voice.

Kit shook her head, already regretting the betrayal of her private restlessness. "Nothing I can't handle."

Ben's lips twisted in a rueful curve of acknowledgment. "Forget I asked," he replied without rancor.

Kit pushed away from the stool where her hip had rested. "I guess I'd better finish my round." Her gaze wandered absently over the slowly emptying room. She gave a faint gasp of surprise as her glance was caught and held by a pair of ebony eyes she remembered all too well.

"What's he doing here?" she asked Ben without breaking the intense visual contact that stretched above the happily unaware patrons seated between them.

"Who?" Ben questioned in response, following the direction of her gaze. "Do you know that guy? He's been here about thirty minutes or so nursing that one Rusty Nail."

"That, my friend, is Harrison Tyler." She nodded in answer to his lifted glass.

"You're kidding," Ben muttered, studying Tyler more carefully. "That's the one Lydia's mom called? No wonder I haven't heard from her. He looks like he could scare the devil out of hell."

Amused at Ben's awed observation, Kit's lips lifted in a gentle curve. "Probably." She turned her head to look at her cousin with a hint of challenge. "Think I can handle him?"

Ben nodded emphatically. "If you can't, it'll be the first time," he pointed out bluntly. "Better you than me right now. With my part in this, I don't need to antagonize him."

"I guess I'd better see what he's doing here."

Taking her time, Kit wove her way toward the far table. As before, greetings assailed her from all sides and she paused periodically to respond in kind. Dan had taught her the value of a good rapport with her clientele. It kept down the fights and disturbances that plagued many of her competitors and had helped Mallory's establish the squeaky clean reputation it enjoyed.

Kit crossed the last few feet to Tyler's chair, conscious of the censuring eyes following her every move. He studied her as though she were a distasteful specimen under a microscope. Kit's annoyance grew with every step. How dare he sit in judgment of her? Who was he to be so blasted self-righteous? He was only an ad executive who created fancy personalities for public figures. His might be a more respectable job, but it was debatable if it was a more honest one.

"Mr. Tyler." She greeted him coolly, her temper firmly under control. Her gaze skimmed the muted blue-toned suit he wore with reluctant appreciation. "What brings you to my place tonight?"

Ignoring her question, Tyler gestured to the empty chair across from him. "Have a seat," he drawled sardonically.

"Will I need to?" Kit responded, eyeing him warily.

Obviously Tyler was in no better mood now than he had been the evening before.

"You weren't so cautious with the rest of your clientele," he pointed out.

Feeling the barb in his comment, Kit's eyes flashed golden sparks. She slipped into the chair to face him fearlessly. "Are you always so extremely unpleasant or is this just an aberration?"

She tilted her chin, her glance sweeping over him with dispassionate interest. In spite of his insulting behavior, her senses registered the beautiful symmetry of his firmly muscled frame. A pullover in cream cable knit hugged his body, accentuating the rich texture of his skin and hair. Although annoyed at herself for noticing, she was still unable to completely subdue her unexpected response to this man.

"Are you always so friendly to the men who spend their money here?" he shot back, his fingers clenching white around the glass he held.

Kit recoiled as though she had been struck, her breath catching audibly in her throat. All sorts of phrases in defense of her right to govern her own actions fought for expression, yet she uttered none of them. The sheer surprise of his suggestive remark momentarily robbed her of the power of speech. She pressed both palms flat on the table, preparing to rise, and inhaled deeply, reminding herself of where she was and the inadvisability of creating a scene. If she remained here one second longer, she was likely to say or do something regrettable even if it would be infinitely satisfying to retaliate.

"We will be closing in ten minutes, so I'll leave you

to finish your drink," she stated in a voice of splintered ice wrapped in silk.

A combination of frustration and self-directed anger shadowed his sternly cast features as he registered her tone. "Kit, I—" he began quickly, using her name for the first time.

"I don't believe I want to hear any more of your comments," Kit interrupted. She stepped back a pace to avoid his hand as it sought to encircle her wrist. "Nor do I wish a scene," she added when he started to get up.

His upward motion halted abruptly. "At least let me apologize," he requested, lowering his voice slightly.

Kit smiled humorlessly, wanting nothing more than to extract herself before she betrayed her anger. "I'll pass, thank you. Ever since I met you, you've been intent on casting me in a disreputable light. I've put up with it and you because of Lydia. But friend, you've just reached the limits of my patience."

"Lydia's the reason I'm here," he inserted swiftly.

Her attention caught—as he had known it would be—Kit hesitated. "And?" she prompted, allowing him the opening but not encouraging anything more than an explanation.

"I was hoping we could get together and discuss the course of action best for Lydia," he admitted, his eyes searching her face for a sign of softening.

Kit's brows rose in undisguised astonishment. "After what you just said and what you obviously think of me! What could I possibly have to contribute? Correct me if I'm wrong, but I thought I was supposed to be the fallen woman leading the innocent astray."

The calculated emphasis Kit had placed on her words found its target with unerring accuracy. His skin darkened and his brows lowered in a straight line over narrowed eyes. Whether his reaction stemmed from anger or embarrassment or a combination of both, Kit neither knew nor cared. Her usually controlled temper was surging past its restraints, invading her body with a tidal wave of anger.

"I'll always be here for Lydia, but for you—" She paused, her gaze an eloquent expression of where he should go and why. "Now if you'll excuse me, I have a few more customers to get friendly with."

She turned on her heel, a practiced smile on her lips for her patrons, to finish her tour of the room. As she stopped here and there to chat, she was vividly aware of the penetrating midnight eyes monitoring her every move. Goaded by a seldom-freed yet characteristic reckless nature, she toyed with the idea of flirting with one of the personable men seated at the bar. It would serve him right if she behaved as the woman he believed her to be. After fleeting consideration, she discarded the idea, realizing that in the end she would suffer more than he.

She concluded her round at the bar. Bracing her hip against the end stool nearest the cash register, she hoped her unwanted customer would go home. With him gone, maybe she could recapture her temper.

"What's the problem?" Ben asked as soon as there was a lull in the final drink orders. "You look like you're ready to singe somebody's tail feathers."

"I already have," she admitted with a sigh.

"Lydia's uncle?" One sandy brow punctuated his concerned question. He glanced briefly at their silent watcher.

She nodded while bestowing a casual good-bye on the newly married couple who were just leaving. It was all she could do to avoid copying Ben's gesture. But no way did she want to capture Tyler's eye again. It was bad enough to feel the searing heat of his concentrated study burning between her shoulder blades without having to see the disapproval in his expression.

"What did he say?" Ben demanded in a mixture of curiosity and anxiety. "Is Lydia all right?"

Kit shrugged, more to dislodge Ty's persistent scrutiny than to answer her cousin's questions. "As far as I know," she responded, suddenly tired. She glanced with seeming disinterest around the room, her gaze passing with careful precision over the shadowed alcove where he sat. "Since things are okay out here, I'm going back to the office to finish up the last of the monthly paperwork." She knew Ben was puzzled over her behavior, but she was past caring. All she wanted at the moment was a retreat from Tyler and his innuendos.

"I'll bring the drawer back after I lock up," Ben offered.

Kit nodded before heading for the corridor where Shadow waited patiently for her return. By the health law, the dog wasn't allowed in the lounge itself, so Kit always left him at the beginning of the passage leading to her office. The big animal rose silently as she reached him and fell into step at her right side. The soft brush of his head against her denim-clad thigh was just the touch of normalcy Kit needed.

What did she care what Harrison Tyler thought of her? If he was so determined to see her as the owner of a saloon in a red-light district, then let him. For a moment the memory of his gentleness with Lydia in the parking lot intruded, dispelling the rigid, judgmental side he showed to her. If only that attractive facet of his personality was a true picture of him, then what a man Harrison Tyler would be.

He had a physical magnetism that drew her while his obvious love and concern for his family struck a sympathetic cord within her. Yet for her he had only insults and barbed words that he aimed with wounding accuracy.

Sighing disappointedly at the prejudice of his nature, Kit entered her office, shutting the door behind her. It was no use wishing for the stars, she reminded herself. She'd run into too many people like him not to realize there was nothing she could do to change his attitude.

Her eyes fell on the small stack of bills she still needed to post in her account book. "If I don't get to work, I'll be here until morning," she murmured aloud, slightly exaggerating her task.

She grimaced at the least favorite of the many jobs connected with the running of Mallory's before settling behind her desk. Shadow curled at her feet as she reached for the next slip awaiting her attention. Working quickly, she noted each sum in the appropriate column. She barely glanced up when Ben appeared with the cash drawer and the evening's receipts.

"I've counted out." He laid the zippered bank bag and the metal register tray on the corner of the desk. "I made up the deposit for you and set the cash up for tomorrow."

"Thanks, Ben." She gestured toward the hidden safe behind her. "How about putting it away for me? And put the bank bag in my carryall."

Without a word, Ben carried out her directions. "I'm on my way," he announced when he was done. "I want to be home early tonight in case Lydia calls."

"She phones you this late?" Kit asked, surprised. She paused in the middle of writing in a total to glance up at him.

"Sometimes, when we haven't seen each other for a day or so." He looked at the key ring he held. "The girls are gone and I've locked up and set the back alarm."

Kit wondered at the odd note she detected in her cousin's voice. "I'll see you Monday," she murmured the automatic good-bye. She half expected another of his lectures on staying in the pub alone. The absence of that, plus the hurried, almost too-casual way he waved himself out of her office brought a curious lift to one brow.

"What was that all about?" she mused aloud, staring at the empty doorway. "I wonder why he looked so guilty." Shaking her head, she returned her attention to the job before her. It was probably her imagination. These last few days had been distinctly unsettling, ending with tonight's scene with Harrison Tyler. He was the one who was guilty, not Ben. Her cousin hadn't a dishonest bone in his body.

"Four hundred thirty-seven dollars and ninety—" Kit mumbled as she wrote in the next amount.

Shadow's growl rumbled a warning, startling Kit into squiggling her seven as she dropped her pencil.

"Easy," she soothed, her right hand swiftly grasping the heavy, tooled-leather collar around his neck. She stared at her open door, rising to her feet in one smooth, silent motion. Her muscles tensed in readiness as she poised, waiting to confront the intruder Shadow's actions told her waited in the corridor.

Her eyes widened when a large dark form stepped from the dark hall into the spill of light illuminating her doorway. "Ty," she breathed in recognition, unconsciously using his family nickname for the first time.

"I came to apologize," he stated quietly, his eyes holding her with an immovable determination. "I can do it from here, but I'd rather sit down so we can talk."

Kit studied him, caught between wanting to toss his words back at him and wishing she dared believe the sincerity she saw in his expression. Beside her, Shadow continued his slow, deep-throated promise of protection when she made no effort to silence him.

"Why?" she demanded finally. "What changed your mind about me? Or is it your bluntness you're apologizing for?"

Ty lifted his hands in an oddly helpless gesture. "How can I answer you without explaining myself?" he questioned in turn. "Will you be fairer than I was and listen?"

The smoothly delivered invitation coupled with the vulnerability of his stance soothed some of Kit's anger. Yet her realistic nature warned her of a possibly calculated attempt on his part to soften her up. The thought was not a pleasant one.

"Put like that, how can I refuse?" she responded finally with a touch of exasperation at his tactics. What was it besides Tyler's physical appeal to her senses that made her want to believe him? She couldn't remember the last time she had taken so much from anyone.

"Well, do I stay here or will you let me come in?" he prompted, his gaze going significantly to the Doberman at her side.

Kit's fingers tightened briefly on Shadow's collar. "It's okay, Shadow, this is a friend." She gentled the dog as she stressed her words with calm emphasis. She glanced at Tyler. "You can come in now. He won't bother you." She walked around the desk, bringing the Doberman with her to stop in front of Tyler. Using the established routine, she introduced the man and the dog to each other.

"He's a good-looking pinscher," he observed. He had given Shadow his hand to sniff, and now he straightened up. "I can see he's well-trained, too."

Kit's eyes flickered slightly at his dry comment. "He's a working dog. He has to be." She gave a quick hand signal, sending the Doberman back to his favorite resting place near her chair. "He's more than a friend, he's my protector if I need one."

"It sounds like I should be glad you identified me as a friend," he replied, staring at her closely.

"Even that won't help you if he feels I'm in difficulties," she warned, aware of the subtle nuance in his velvety voice, yet unsure of its significance. She gestured toward the visitor's chair.

He ignored her invitation to sit down.

"I've made you distrust me, haven't I?" He shook his head, his expression alive with self-disgust. "Believe it or not, I'm not usually so objectionable."

"That's a relief," Kit responded, unable to resist the small sarcastic dig.

Tyler stepped forward a pace until his body was only inches from hers. "Can we start again?"

"Why?" she asked bluntly, sternly suppressing a desire to agree without questioning his motives.

He hesitated, his gaze sliding away for a moment before returning to hold hers steadily. "Because of Lydia and her need for you," he answered finally.

Disappointment, pure and surprisingly strong, rippled through Kit at his words. Even as she recognized her reaction, she pushed it from her mind and forced herself to concentrate on the relief she should be feeling.

"No more prejudiced digs about my work?" she said slowly.

He shook his head. "Or you either," he added. He lifted his hand to her cheek in a strangely intimate gesture. "I hurt you earlier. I never meant to do that."

Mesmerized by the husky admission and the warmth of his fingers against her skin, Kit stared at him in unblinking concentration. Where was her anger, her sense of ill-usage? With only a few words he had breached her barriers to such a degree that she was allowing him to touch her. The black of his eyes was like an ebony cloak of night surrounding her in a silence alive with sensation. His breathing was the sighing of the evening breeze, the heat of his body the warmth of the sun-toasted earth against the cooler night clime.

"No answer?" he prompted, still in the whispered rumble that rolled gently over her ears. His gaze flowed over her beautifully contoured face, the generous mouth and the honesty in her sherry eyes. "I'm trying hard to see beyond what I thought you should be. I don't want to believe you're cynical or disreputable. Won't you meet me halfway? You took Lydia in."

Kit started slightly at the mention of the girl and the problem between them. For a moment, she had almost forgotten who Ty was and what his reasons were for being with her.

"I'll try," she agreed, backing slowly away from his caressing fingers.

"Good. Will you have dinner with me tomorrow?"

"I can't," Kit answered without thinking. The unexpectedness of his request threw her off balance for a moment.

"We really need to talk. I've spoken with Lydia, but it hasn't done much good," he returned reasonably, making no move to close the distance between them.

Kit stared at a point beyond his left shoulder, trying to decide what she wanted to do. Tyler was entirely too attractive to risk seeing in a social setting while Lydia and Ben stood between them. Honesty made her admit she seemed to have little control where her reactions to him were concerned. Yet she couldn't refuse to see him—not while Lydia and Ben needed her and the sympathetic support she could bring to the situation. Thinking of her cousin's plight, she knew she shouldn't put off the meeting.

"I'm going to a barbecue tomorrow but I should be home by six." She focused on his face, reading nothing more than polite interest. "Why don't you stop by my place about seven?"

"I'll be there," he agreed immediately and took down her address. He turned to stride toward the door then hesitated, looking back over his shoulder. "This time I promise I won't jump to conclusions."

Kit watched him walk out, her eyes wide with amazement. For a brief moment, his expression had held an odd determination totally out of keeping with his softly spoken promise. What was driving him to take a course of action that he obviously found difficult? Was it only his concern for Lydia? Or was it possible that he, too, was caught in the trap of physical awareness? She had noticed more than one spark of interest in his eyes.

4

Kit slipped out of her car, her sandaled feet making no sound on the carpet of dried pine needles. Before her stretched a narrow path beaten into the sand by countless feet that lead to a large, two-story houseboat. The floating home nudged gently at its mooring lines, sending flashes of reflected sunlight off the windows to illuminate the shade beneath the Australian pines where she stood.

"I thought it was you." Summer Marshall strolled from the shadowy interior of the bait shop toward her. A welcoming smile lit her face and sparked her amber eyes with flecks of gold dust.

"I don't think I want to know you," Kit greeted her long-legged friend with a grin. "You're looking disgustingly gorgeous as usual."

Summer laughed, her gaze traveling over her own

denim cutoffs and well-worn T-shirt with a fond eye. "It feels so good to get back here. Boston's beautiful, but Jupiter's still my favorite place to be."

Kit nodded, easily understanding Summer's appreciation of the more relaxed life-style of her home. "So where are Brandon and the kids?" she asked, glancing around.

"Gone to the store to get some charcoal," Summer explained with a suitably straight face.

"Brandon?" Kit's skeptical expression echoed her amazement. "I can't believe it. In fact, I'm not sure I can even imagine him coping with a teenager and a toddler."

Summer tucked her arm through Kit's, urging her toward the gangway of the houseboat. "Now don't you go maligning my husband. I'll have you know he's super with the baby and Shannon worships the ground he walks on."

Kit shook her head, having difficulty picturing the aloof Brandon in the guise Summer described. Anyone less like a family man couldn't exist. "Something tells me I missed a lot when you two decided to stay in Boston last year."

Summer pushed open the door, allowing Kit to precede her inside. "We're very happy," she admitted huskily, all humor gone from her features. She led the way up the spiral stairway to the second floor. "Shall we go out onto the deck? I've got strawberry daiquiries in the fridge. Do you want one?" She moved gracefully to the small open kitchen and the gleaming white refrigerator.

"Yes to both," Kit agreed absently as she studied Summer curiously. "Can I ask you something?"

Summer glanced up, a pitcher of frothy pink liquid in one hand. "Sure," she replied, her eyes registering Kit's uncharacteristically hesitant tone. "Just let me pour this into two glasses and then I'm all yours." Suiting her words to actions, she quickly prepared their drinks and handed one to Kit.

"Now, tell me what's got you so unsettled," Summer demanded when they'd each taken a seat on the soft, cushioned deck chairs.

Startled at her friend's perceptive description of her frame of mind, Kit stared out across the water, trying to gather her thoughts. For a fleeting moment, she regretted the impulse that had prompted her to seek Summer's opinion.

"If you're wishing you hadn't said anything, I'll understand," Summer offered quietly in the silence. She watched Kit's face, reading the indecision written clearly on the normally serene features.

Kit turned to meet her eyes. "Have you ever wondered why we seem to mesh so well? I've never known another person, with the exception of Dan, that I could speak to so freely. It's only been three years since Brandon introduced us."

"Right after our marriage, in fact," Summer murmured, her voice filled with memories. "Sometimes it seems like only yesterday."

For a moment neither spoke as each relived the surprise Brandon's wedding had caused, the speculation, and finally the instant friendship the two women had felt. A tie that neither distance nor the short visits had weakened.

Kit sighed as she came slowly back to the present and the sun-drenched scene before her.

"His name is Harrison Tyler and he's the uncle of that girl I wrote you about," Kit began, her gaze fixed firmly on the lighthouse across the inlet. "He disapproves of me and my association with Lydia."

"And it matters?" Summer interjected, easily reading between the lines.

Kit turned her head to snag Summer's gentle golden eyes. "Physically he appeals to me more than any man I've ever known," she replied, indirectly answering Summer's question. "But mentally he's eons away from what I look for in a man. He's judgmental and prejudiced and now he wants to see me to talk about Lydia." Kit surged to her feet, driven by a sudden need to expend some of the chaos inside of her. "When he touches me, I want to lean on him, to melt right into his body until we're one." She whirled around, her eyes dark with her troubled thoughts. "I've never felt like this about anyone. And damned if I know what to do."

"I gather from that remark that you want him."

"Yes. Dumb, isn't it, considering I'm involved in this problem with Lydia." She paused, then quickly explained the latest developments, including Lydia's lies and hers and Ben's relationship. "What a situation," she ended with a sigh.

Summer whistled softly in surprise. "That's a good word for it," she agreed, her brow wrinkling as she considered the implications. "What about Ben? How's he taking it?"

"How do you think?" Kit snapped irritably. "Sorry." Her apologetic mutter floated between them, emphasizing her loss of control.

"And you're asking me what to do?" Summer's brows lifted skeptically. "To tell you the truth, I haven't a clue." She raised her drink to her lips to take a sip. "Does the uncle know the whole story?"

Kit shook her head. "Ben wants to tell him, but I was hoping if we gave Lydia a little time, she'd do it herself."

"And if she doesn't?"

Kit shrugged before flinging herself down in her chair. "Then Ben will, but in the meantime both of us are living a lie."

"And with Ty's already bad opinion, you're in a no-win situation."

"Got it in one," Kit agreed bluntly. "Blast the man. Why can't I get him out of my mind?"

"You sound like I did when I first met Brandon. He positively plagued my dreams." Summer gazed at the home that had once been hers alone.

"But you married your man. You know I'm not interested in anything so permanent," Kit responded.

"I never have understood why you're so anti-marriage," Summer probed delicately.

"It's not so much that I'm antimarriage, it's just that I like my life the way it is. I have my own business with no one to answer to but myself. I travel, I live in my own place. In short, I don't have to consider someone else's wants and needs. A self-indulgent way of thinking, but there it is."

"You may be a lot of things, Kit Mallory, but self-indulgent isn't one of them," Summer stated with a conviction born of personal knowledge of Kit's caring attitude toward others. "A selfish person doesn't help out troubled strangers or see that overindulgent customers are sent home in taxis, sometimes even at her own expense."

Although warmed by Summer's defense, Kit shrugged dismissively. "That's just good business."

"What's good business?"

The intrusion of the deep, masculine voice drew both women's attention to the man standing in the sliding-glass doorway leading from the family room to the deck. A dark-haired toddler, a younger version of Brandon Marshall, was held comfortably against one broad shoulder.

"Hello, Kit." Brandon greeted their visitor with a slight smile of welcome lighting his often-photographed features. He strolled over to deposit his son in Summer's waiting arms. "Remind me not to take this little monster with me to the grocery store again. Do you know he lightfingers anything that takes his eye?"

Summer grinned unrepentently at her husband. "Did you catch him before or after the cashier?"

Momentarily forgotten by her hosts, Kit followed the homey interchange with amazement. As often as she had witnessed the changes in Brandon since his marriage, she still found it difficult to believe the way he was now compared to what she knew him to be in the past. The handsome nomad who roamed the world at will had been transformed into a caring man capable of great love for the golden-eyed woman he had wed, her daughter, Shannon and their son, Jason.

Kit often wondered when she saw the four of them together if Brandon ever missed his old life. Yet try as she would, she could find no sign that he did. And much as she hated to admit it, his attitude bothered her; in an odd way, Brandon's freedom-loving ways reminded her too much of her own. Until Summer, he had always trod his own path, alone and unfettered, just as she did. Now, though, it appeared that was all at an end, and he apparently was glad that it should be so.

"Kit, where are you?"

Summer's teasing question interrupted Kit's thoughts, bringing her back to the present. "Sorry," Kit apologized quickly, dividing her glance between the two pairs of eyes gazing at her with varying degrees of speculation in their depths. "Where's Shannon?" The question was a small evasion on Kit's part, but she was past caring. She was tired of the haunting restlessness eroding her peace. She wanted an end to it and she needed to enjoy this interlude before she had to face the complex problem of Harrison Tyler.

"She's on the beach setting up the grill," Brandon answered after a short pause. "I'd better get down there and get the coals started or we won't eat until late tonight." He bent to drop a kiss on Summer's upturned lips. "Shall I take Jason with me?"

Summer shook her head. "We'll take care of him.

You just handle the steaks." Her gaze followed him lovingly as he strolled away. "Even after three years, I still find it hard to believe we're married." She turned to Kit, a soft glow of love touching her with beauty. "I bet you find it difficult too, since you've known him so long."

Startled at Summer's unconscious mirroring of her own thoughts, Kit hesitated briefly before inclining her head in agreement. "The first time my stepfather introduced him to me, I was as awestruck as any teenager with her first crush. Even then he had a reputation for jet-setting, for being a free spirit, although no one called it that in those days." She laughed lightly at her memories. "I can remember deciding that one day I would make my own way, see the world and do whatever intrigued me. I envied him his freedom, though never his money." She shifted uneasily in her chair. "I've done just about everything I set out to do. I've traveled, tried windsurfing, skydiving and even a spot of white-water rafting. I own one of the most popular night spots in this part of Florida."

"And?" Summer prompted gently.

Kit stared at her friend and the child she held against her breast. "I don't know." She lifted her hands in a helpless gesture. "I'm not bored, frustrated or discontented."

"How about empty?"

Kit's brows rose skeptically. "With my schedule, I don't have time for that problem."

"When's the last time you shared yourself with someone?"

Kit shrugged, unsurprised at Summer's straight talk.

"Almost a year," she murmured after a moment's consideration. "I know what you're getting at, but I hardly think a short-term relationship is the cure for this."

Summer rose gracefully, perching her son securely on one hip. "How about a long-term commitment like marriage?"

"Not for someone like me," Kit denied flatly.

"It worked for Brandon," she pointed out inarguably.

Kit got to her feet, her eyes reflecting her troubled state. "You two are a special case. I can't think of one person in my life who affects me the way either of you touch the other."

"What about Harrison Tyler?" Summer demanded.

Kit's lips curled in a twisted smile. "He gets to me, all right. Only it's sex, pure and simple physical attraction."

Summer hesitated, studying her carefully. "Are you sure?"

Kit reached for the surprisingly silent child on Summer's hip, suddenly needing a diversion. "I'm certain. I told you, the man doesn't like me or what I do." She hugged the small body close for a moment, exchanging an absent smile with the child.

Summer opened her mouth to argue the point, then shut it abruptly, obviously having thought better of interfering. "Let's get this picnic on the road. I don't know about you, but I'm starving."

Relieved at Summer's change of subject, Kit made an effort to throw off her mood as she followed Summer to the kitchen. The arrival of leggy, fourteen-year-old Shannon, demanding the steaks for grilling, helped ease the slight awkwardness she felt. From that moment on the day became a quiet celebration with good friends and delicious food, sprinkled with bits of fun, teasing and laughter. The tightrope show Shannon put on, walking up the thick mooring line securing the houseboat to a piling on the beach, the theft of one beautifully cooked T-bone by the family dog, Sailor, and the look on Brandon's face when his son liberally painted his father's shirtfront with catsup-coated hands were all happy memories Kit knew she'd hold for a long time.

She drove home later that afternoon pleasantly tired from the game of touch football they'd played on the beach. She got out of her car, smiling at the splattered, sandy-coated image she presented. Brandon hadn't been the only one to benefit from Jason's nimble, food-smeared fingers. Shadow woofed a greeting, nosing her eagerly as she let herself into her apartment.

"Down, you big ox," she commanded, barely managing to evade his long, damp tongue as he tried to lick her face. "I'm all sticky and you just had your weekly bath this morning, so behave."

Recognizing the mention of his least favorite pastime, Shadow subsided with a reproachful look in his liquid brown eyes. Chuckling at his almost human expression, Kit headed for her bedroom and a much-needed shower. Music from the stereo she switched on before entering the bathroom enveloped her as she stood beneath the warm spray. The strains of the

Chariots of Fire soundtrack, with its ocean melody, were a soothing accompaniment to the water flowing over her body. Squeezing a little of her aqua shower gel on her bath sponge, Kit cleansed away the souvenirs of her afternoon.

When she had rinsed, she stepped out of the stall to wrap her lightly scented body in a thick burgundy velour bath sheet. Droplets of water clung to her shoulders like a sprinkling of diamonds on satin flesh. Releasing her waist-length hair from the braid coiled atop her head, she brushed her auburn mane with long strokes until it lay against her back in a shiny swath.

Padding back into her bedroom, she stopped in front of her closet, trying to decide what to wear. Her at-home clothes were a decided contrast to her ultra-conservative, almost sexless, work wardrobe. Her love of vibrant colors and her eye for well-cut designs had resulted in a collection of daring, provocative outfits.

She stared indecisively at the two different images available to her for a full minute. Then she reached for the most exotic leisure creation she owned, a reckless sparkle flaring to life in her sherry eyes. She never had been one to opt for safety over possible danger. In fact, as Dan had once remarked, she had the looks of an angel and a streak of pure Satan when the mood was on her.

And tonight it definitely was burning within her, she decided, surveying the clingy, emerald swirl of fabric draped around her curves. The fine gauze cotton was a floor-length wraparound styled to end in a soft looping tie between the wearer's breasts. Tiny, carefully hidden hooks closed the resulting slit down to knee level. Yet, for all its modest design, it gave the illusion of defying gravity with its backless, strapless appearance. A man could be forgiven for wondering how it stayed in place.

Closing her mind to the possible consequences of wearing such a dress, Kit braided her hair in its usual long plait, entwining a single strand of emerald ribbon in the thick cord; then she applied light makeup. She stood before the full-length mirror on the inside of her closet door and surveyed her reflection. Bare feet with bronze-tinted toenails peeked out beneath the emerald hem, adding a casual note in keeping with her simple hairstyle.

"Not bad," she murmured, pleased with her effort. Harrison Tyler had condemned the bar owner; now let's see if he condemns the woman.

She strolled out of her room to the kitchen to pour herself a glass of white wine. The doorbell chimed just as she opened the bottle. Placing it on the counter, she went to answer Tyler's summons, unsurprised at his punctuality. Somehow she'd known he would honor his commitments, no matter how small they were. Ty was leaning against the doorjamb looking just as attractive as she remembered when she opened the door.

A light blue short-sleeved shirt encased his upper body, accentuating the firm muscles of his arms and chest. Dark navy slacks rode low on his hips and faithfully followed the straight length of his legs. He presented a casual picture. Yet there was a raw, vaguely untamed quality about him that called to Kit, making her vividly aware of her own femininity. And doubly glad she had chosen to wear one of her favorite outfits.

Sternly commanding her senses to behave and her wits to remain sharp, she stepped back to allow him to enter. "I was just about to pour myself a glass of Asti Spumante. Would you like one?"

"Yes." His rapier glance moved slowly over her body, settling at last on her serenely composed face. "Why on earth do you wear those sexless clothes at your pub?" he breathed huskily. "With a figure like yours . . ." He shook his head as his voice trailed away.

Kit stared at him for a long moment, startled not by what he had said but by the expression in his eyes. She had seen desire in a man's eyes before, but nothing like the naked wanting blazing in the night-dark depths of his gaze. And the fact that he made no effort to disguise or hide his hunger bothered her even more because of the unexpectedness of his response. Except for that one gentle touch at their last meeting and the faint interest she had observed in him once or twice, Tyler had seemed completely oblivious to her as a woman. But now he appeared very aware of her.

Which reaction was the true one? she wondered, feeling a shiver of excitement ripple along her spine. It had been a long time since a man had affected her so strongly. Suddenly unable to resist the challenge he represented, Kit decided to enjoy a taste of the attraction she felt. She didn't dare allow herself what she really wanted, but surely there was no harm in a small sample.

With that in mind, she corralled her vividly responsive senses and retreated behind her cool, tranquil public image. From this safe haven she could view events as they transpired, choosing her own time to involve herself.

"I dress for the pub to avoid comments like that one," she explained calmly into the long silence. "Considering your opinion of my business, I would have thought you would realize that."

"I'm not going to be forgiven for that first impression, am I?" Ty murmured, watching her closely through half-closed eyes. "Couldn't you put my attitude down to a worried, frustrated man's reaction in a situation with which he had no experience?"

Kit tilted her head, considering the softly cajoling request. If she closed her eyes and let herself believe in the soothing, faintly pleading voice that seemed to reach out and stroke her ears, she probably would do just as he asked. But, unfortunately for him, she had her eyes wide open and could see the carefully masked determination in the set of his jaw and the watchful glitter in the partially screened dark eyes.

"I'll think about it," she drawled slowly, as though she was doing just that. The challenge of pitting her wits against this man sang in her veins. The stakes were high but, oh, the rewards for Lydia, for Ben, and just possibly for her, too, were great.

"Will you risk a drink with me?"

"Yes," he agreed simply, smiling faintly, which might have been meant to be reassuring but wasn't.

The controlled tension in his body was a dead giveaway. The hunger in his eyes still lingered, but now it was overlaid with speculation, curiosity and an odd gleam of something Kit couldn't quite put a name to. Could it be that he too felt the same hint of dangerous exhilaration she knew at the prospect of the coming encounter?

5

~~~~~~~~

So what did you want to talk to me about?" Kit asked, her gaze focused on the light-colored liquid in her tulip-shaped wineglass. She tucked her feet more comfortably beneath her and settled back into the plush champagne cushions of the sofa. The edge of her line of sight cataloged Tyler's reactions as he sat in seeming relaxation at the other end of the couch.

"I'm hoping you can give me some answers," he explained slowly. He raised his glass to take a short swallow before continuing. "To be honest, I need your help."

Kit lifted her head with a startled snap, her eyes flying to meet his. "You surprise me."

"I shouldn't. I think you know how difficult it is to talk to Lydia these days and, believe me, Emily's not much better. So far, I've been treated to a list of grievances it would take the UN to solve." He grimaced in remembered disgust. "Except for them, you're the only other person who seems to know the facts. And you don't strike me as someone who's going to dwell on petty wrongs without ever getting to the real problem."

"Thank you, I think, for the compliment." Kit sipped her wine thoughtfully as she gathered her thoughts for the coming explanation. It was important that she present her knowledge in the most sympathetic light possible. Lydia deserved her support and Ben needed Tyler's goodwill. Not that she could mention Ben's total involvement, but maybe she could pave the way for him a bit.

"Lydia first started coming to the pub three months ago. She'd arrive alone, shortly after we opened and stay till closing."

"She drank all those hours?" Tyler demanded, his jaw clenching in a visible effort to restrain his temper. "Didn't anyone think her behavior odd?"

Understanding his anger and the concern behind it, Kit ignored the implied slur on their actions. "Ben, my bartender, did from the first night. Mainly because he knows it's a policy of the house to keep watch over unescorted females for obvious reasons. Even when he decided Lydia wasn't waiting around to pick up a man, he still kept an eye on her and finally, after the fourth night in a row, he came to me." She paused, carefully editing Ben's personal interest in the beautiful blonde out of her next words. "I had noticed your niece and after hearing Ben's account, I decided to talk to her if she came in again."

Now that she was past the worst of Ben's initial involvement, Kit related the bare facts of Lydia's state of mind, her rebellion at her mother's determined efforts to police her movements, her disillusionment over her adored father's desertion months before and her feelings of abandonment since her mother began a demanding new career as a real estate broker. "She was all set to drop out of school, get a job and leave home," she finished bluntly.

"Damn," Tyler swore, raking a hand through his hair in a gesture of frustration. "Why didn't she call me? Why didn't either of them call, instead of waiting until things got this bad?"

"At a guess, I'd say it was pride on both your sister's and Lydia's parts. From what Lydia has said her mother believes in handling her own problems. Lydia even admires the way Emily refused your offer to help support them. I think Lydia's secretly proud of her mother's success. I think unconsciously she's trying to be as strong as her mother. Only her youth is getting in the way, making her bid for independence take the guise of rebellion."

"I thought it was bartenders who were the armchair psychologists," he cut in with a frown of annoyance at her outspoken opinion.

"You came to me for help," Kit pointed out swiftly. "I can stop any time you want. Or sooner, if you don't watch your insults." She glared at him, making no effort to hide her temper. "For your information, I wasn't indulging in some stupid game of amateur analysis. My comments are based solely on my own experience with a situation very similar to Lydia's and with a mother who was trying her best to provide a living for us both."

The silence following her outburst was total. Kit stared at Ty, ready to tell him to leave if he said one more objectionable word.

"It looks like all I do is put my foot in my mouth where you're concerned. I'd go down on my knees if I thought it would wipe out the last few minutes, but it won't. And the damnable part of this is that I can't honestly promise I won't step on your toes again." He hesitated awkwardly, searching her unchanging expression. "Do you have any idea how difficult this is for me? I've got two emotional females on my hands. I'm a bachelor with no experience with parenting and I'm being cast in a pseudo-paternal role. And you're supposed to be the villain of the piece, leading my innocent niece down the path to ruin. Only you don't appear to be that at all. Instead you're everything I'd want Lydia to find in a confidante—sympathetic yet clear-sighted and unashamedly honest." He laughed humorlessly at the unconcealed surprise flickering across Kit's face. "Don't look so shocked. Lydia has managed to impart some of your advice to her."

"If all that's true, then why do you keep on attacking me?"

He shrugged evasively before getting restlessly to his feet. He set his empty glass on the coffee table in front of the couch, then jammed his hands in his pockets. He glanced down at her, his eyes reflecting his troubled thoughts.

"Frustration and anger at this mess. Perhaps even a little jealousy that Lydia would confide in a stranger before she did her own family," he murmured. "Not very noble reactions, are they?"

Kit shook her head, her gaze softening with compassion at the pain she saw in the depths of his eyes. With that vulnerability and the effort it had cost him to be open with her, Kit found the one-dimensional physical attraction she felt for him deepen with respect and admiration. It took a very special person to be strong enough to admit his faults.

"Who wants a noble man, anyway?" she offered gently. "He would probably be a dead bore to have around."

Her lightly teasing comment drew a startled look. For a split second he stared at her as though he couldn't believe his ears. Then in the blink of an eye, his serious expression dissolved into a network of fine lines of laughter as he began to chuckle. The rich rumble of his amusement reached out to Kit, beckoning her to join in the tension-breaker.

"No wonder every sentence Lydia utters begins with 'Kit says,'" he retorted, taking his seat again.

He lounged back against the cushions, feeling suddenly at ease. His gaze trailed over Kit's still figure, following the daring drape of her gown and the satiny flesh it embraced. Yet in spite of the obviously eye-riveting dimensions of her curves, it was the serenity of her face that held his attention.

Had it been only a moment before that he had seen the flash of angry fire in her unusual eyes? Where was the vivid flare of emotion that made her skin glow with color and her breasts undulate with the force of her heightened breathing? Who was she, this woman who had compassion for a troubled girl and yet owned and ran one of the largest and most popular bars in the area? Her eyes held the knowledge of Eve, her body the allure of Circe and her mind the probing truth of one who looks beyond the surface. She was unique. An intriguing, complex creature beyond the realm of any other female he had ever known.

"Looking for my secrets?" Kit murmured huskily, meeting his intense study with one of her own. His puzzlement, the curiosity he felt was reflected in his eyes. There were questions too, questions she sensed he would ask one day, but not tonight. Tonight was for others, not for them.

Tyler shook his head, physically breaking the silent contact they shared. "There isn't time now," he replied huskily, tacitly admitting there might be in the future. "Lydia must be my main concern."

Kit nodded slightly, her lashes dropping for a brief heartbeat to hide the gleam of anticipation that surged through her. In that moment the restlessness that had plagued her was gone. The challenge Ty represented rose on the horizon to merge with the intricate tangle of lives that had drawn them together. But before she could succumb to its allure, she had to do what she could for Ben and Lydia.

She opened her eyes, all expression except for concern for the present situation removed from the rich sherry depths. "What will you do about Lydia? She needs you and Emily in spite of all her rebelliousness."

"I know she does and, believe it or not, so does my sister. Right now, I can only stay here until Wednesday morning; then I have to be back in Jacksonville until the following Monday. After that, I can arrange my schedule to spend a couple of weeks with them to help straighten things out." He lifted his hands, signaling for silence when Kit would have spoken. "It's not the best plan, I know, but it's the only one I've got."

"I wasn't going to criticize you," Kit defended herself. "In fact, I intended to compliment you. It can't be easy to take an extended leave like this at a moment's notice." She paused, then probed delicately. "What about your sister? Lydia has told me enough about her life in the last few months for me to realize how seldom Lydia and she are together. No matter how close you and Lydia have been in the past, she needs her mother now more than ever."

"Emily knows the score and she intends to do her part," he replied firmly, an underlying strength of purpose in his voice.

Hearing it, Kit wondered if Lydia's mother was only giving her grudging attention to the problem. "This isn't going to work if Lydia senses it's some kind of trick," she warned, frowning at the jarring note she detected. In her business she had to be able to read people by their expressions, vocal inflections and body language. Through years of practice, she had developed that tool into a fine art. There was something out of sync in Ty's attitude. Some little piece was missing. Could he have found out about Ben already, she wondered when she failed to find an answer to the puzzle.

"It won't be a trick," he assured her after a short pause. He glanced away, then back to her again, pinning her with a dark rapier-sharp stare. "Emily wants you out of the picture."

Kit's eyes widened at the blunt demand. For a moment, she was struck dumb with the absolutely senseless insensitivity shown by such a command.

"It's not personal," he added quickly, then stopped. "Damn." The oath ripped out of him, catching him unaware. He had meant to put their plan to her gently; instead he had blurted it out like some tactless fool. Where was all the smooth charm he had cultivated over the years to soothe temperamental clients?

"No, I don't imagine it is personal," Kit agreed evenly while every nerve in her body protested at the stillness she needed to control her resentment. "After all, I've never met Emily, have I?" She rose, holding her glass. "I think I need a refill. How about you?"

Tyler picked up his glass to give it to her. As Kit's hand curved around the bowl, his free hand encircled her wrist. "Look at me," he ordered.

Kit stared at the lean fingers wrapped around her slender wrist, then focused on his determined face. "I don't like being caged, not by bars or by people," she stated clearly, giving her arm the slightest of significant shakes. "My freedom, please." Sherry eyes met black in their first clear-cut battle for power.

He had no right, Tyler acknowledged, catching the sharp reprimand in her gaze. And yet he couldn't let her go on thinking what he knew she had to be. How could he explain how insecure his usually capable sister was feeling? How threatened she was by Kit's influence with her daughter? Would Kit's understanding stretch that far in the light of the judgmental remarks he had made about her business? Slowly, he relaxed his fingers one by one, until only the faintest imprint of his grip remained on the smooth, velvet-soft skin.

"Will you let me explain?" he asked, not really surprised to hear an unaccustomed note of coaxing in his voice. When she remained where she was, he felt his tense muscles relax slightly. Although she was wary, she hadn't completely refused him.

"I won't deny part of Emily's objection is based on what you do. But more importantly, she fears you've usurped her role in Lydia's life. And so do I. Emily needs her daughter just as much as Lydia needs her mother. And you're between them. Can't you see that?"

"No, I'm not, because I've been very careful not to infringe on any ties Lydia has with either of you," Kit disagreed emphatically. "The only thing I've done is to offer Lydia a place off the streets and out of bars and a willing ear to listen to her troubles. Any advice I've given her has been to talk to one or both of you about her feelings. Whether either of you believe it or not, I've never once criticized your handling of Lydia. If anything, I've tried to give her an understanding of your points of view." Kit held his gaze with unflinching directness, armored with the truth of her words and actions.

Tyler read the strength in her, the belief she had in herself. Suddenly he found himself wondering just why she had befriended his niece. Why had she put up with his past all-too-obvious disapproval? How did she know how to handle the situation with the delicacy she had shown? In her position, she could have easily caused an even greater rift between Lydia and himself and his sister.

"Why do you care so much?" he asked, driven by the desire to know this intriguingly complex woman better.

Kit didn't answer for a moment as she considered whether or not she wanted to reply. After all, in spite of her growing knowledge of this man, he was still a stranger to her. Did she really want to give him a glimpse into her past now? To allow him to see her at one of her most vulnerable moments?

"I'll refill these," she murmured, temporarily avoiding the issue. The faint flicker of puzzlement in his expression bothered her, although he made no overt move to stop her as she headed for the kitchen.

She poured more wine in their glasses, annoyed with herself for procrastinating. The way she was acting, anyone would think she was afraid to tell him of her own troubled youth. But she knew that wasn't so. She'd never been ashamed of her past. Rather, she'd always felt a sense of pride in herself for coming to grips with her problems, and in those she loved for helping her with their patience and kindness. She reentered the living room with a brimming crystal in each hand, her decision made. She placed his on the table in front of him before curling comfortably in her corner of the sofa.

"Lydia and I have a lot in common. The difference between us really lies in the age at which we each rebelled. I never knew my father, while Lydia's deserted her and Emily. My mother worked hard to support us, too, and I was just as demanding as Lydia. I couldn't accept her hours, her lack of interest in me, which was due more to tiredness than indifference. So I became a juvenile hell-raiser. I was in trouble at school, drinking and smoking. And believe me, for a thirteen-year-old in my generation, that was very bad." Kit lifted her glass to her lips to savor the delicate taste against her tongue. It, like the advent of Dan in her young life, dispelled some of the memory of those unhappy times.

"Then I met Dan Mallory, my mother's new employer, and the man who later became my stepfather. Where my mother had failed to reach me, Dan succeeded. Not by tearful reproaches or pleas, but with what they nowadays call 'tough love.'" She smiled gently, remembering her adolescent shock at her adopted parent's blunt appraisal of her and her open warfare. "He treated my complaints to a fair hearing without once pointing out how incredibly selfish I was being. Instead of yapping at me about what I owed my mother, like everyone else had done, he showed me what I owed myself. Things like an education and a job that would support me comfortably, none of which I could get on the streets."

Kit grinned, her eyes sparkling with humor. "It was a good four years before I saw how well he had maneuvered me. And by then it was too late to change. I had become smart enough to see beyond the end of my own nose. I had found out what a remarkable woman my mother was and how well she had done for us." She took a healthy swallow of her drink before she met his strangely softened gaze. "So you see, I wouldn't hurt Lydia or her mother. Not only because of my own past, but also because of the debt I owe Dan. I can never give him back what he gave me, but I can pass on his gift—to Lydia if you'll let me help."

Transfixed by the poignancy of her story as well as the hypnotic pleading in her liquid eyes, Tyler made no sound, no move to break the silence. Whatever lingering doubts he'd had about this woman were gone. No one could fake the depth of emotion her words held nor the pain of an adolescence that was so like Lydia's.

"Thank you for telling me," he said simply. "I'll talk to Emily so she'll understand."

Kit nodded, releasing the breath she had hardly been aware of holding in a soft sigh. "In return I promise you that if Lydia's with me, she won't be in my bar," she replied, giving him the only assurance she could guarantee. The mellowness of his mood almost tempted her to risk telling him of Ben's involvement. Now, more than ever, she disliked the subterfuge she was using to keep Ben and Lydia's relationship quiet.

Nodding his acceptance, Tyler picked up his drink and finished it in a few swallows. "I've taken up enough of your evening," he murmured. "And aside from that, I've got to talk to Emily tonight, before she tackles Lydia."

Kit rose, taking his words at face value. She walked with him to the door where Shadow lay sleeping on the cool foyer tiles.

"Will you call me and let me know how it goes?"

she asked without stopping to think how her request would sound.

Tyler's teeth gleamed briefly in a small smile. The dim light of the hallway traced shadows over the sharp outline of his bold features, surrounding them with a mysterious aura. "Would you have dinner with me instead?"

"What?" Kit exclaimed, too startled at the sudden request to guard her tongue. Why hadn't she expected it, she wondered, remembering the flashes of awareness between them.

Ty smiled faintly. "My timing must be incredibly off," he observed, the beginning of amusement lighting his onyx eyes. He lifted his hand slowly as though he were afraid of startling her. His fingers drifted lightly around her throat to stroke the smooth column and the pulsing throb in its hollow. "Any place you say," he added beguilingly, making no effort to hide his anxiousness for her agreement.

"This doesn't make sense," Kit objected, fighting the traitorous urge to lean into his soothing caress.

"I think it makes perfect sense," he disagreed in a husky whisper. "What better way to share our thoughts and pool our resources to help Lydia?"

Kit stared at him, torn between the awakening needs of her body and the realistic wariness of her mind. There was so much he still didn't know. And when he found out—? But oh how good it felt when he touched her. The deep ripple of his voice curled around her senses, enticing her to forget her caution. The scent of him teased at her, beckoning her to risk spending time with him.

"All right," she breathed finally, her voice revealing her ambivalence.

"Good," he groaned huskily. He bent his head until his lips brushed hers softly, then drew back to hover just out of reach. "I've been wanting to do that ever since I walked in tonight."

"Ty, this is crazy," Kit protested, struggling to escape the slowly tightening mesh of attraction drawing her ever closer. She splayed her fingers against his chest.

"Don't fight me, honey. I only want a small taste now."

The promise his words held for the future brought Kit's head up sharply. He was much too sure of himself, she decided, as an angry reprimand formed on her lips.

In the next second, her rebuttal was blocked in her throat as he covered her lips with his. Kit dug her nails into the light fabric of his shirt in an instinctive move to stop him and to keep her balance. Neither effort was successful. He simply ignored the tiny wedge and gathered her into his arms, trapping her hands between them.

Assailed by a variety of sensations, Kit's defenses crumbled after a brief battle. How easily her body responded to his touch. The flavor of the drink they'd shared mingled with the moist warmth of his mouth to create an intoxicating feast for her suddenly hungry tongue. Kit was vividly aware of each hard plane and contour of Ty's body. In spite of the barrier of her imprisoned arms, her breasts were crushed against his smoothly muscled chest. Her hips arched into the hardening line of his lower body as he braced his legs to take her weight against him. She was caged by his eager mouth and encircling embrace and held fast between his strong thighs. And reveling in her captivity. Never had she known such masculine aggression, yet she felt no threat, only a sense of her own female power.

"I knew you would feel like this," he grated against her mouth. "Soft." His hands slid up her shoulders, lightly stroking the willow-slim curves before settling at the nape of her neck. "Warm, so feminine, too."

"Me, a lady bar owner?" Kit managed to interject, striving to bring her pulse rate and her emotions under control.

"You're not going to let me forget, are you?" he demanded, nibbling at the corner of her mouth. "I've apologized."

"So you have," she agreed with a faint breathlessness. Unless she stopped him now, she might be unable to in a moment. "But you can't expect me to fully trust your motives. I'm not available if all you need is a woman, any woman."

Ty's hands tightened on her at her words. His fingers closed around her collarbone as he held her away from him. "Is that what you think?" he muttered, staring at her intently as though he would probe the secrets of her mind. "I'll admit I've given you no reason to believe in my good opinion of you, but I damn well don't think I deserve that."

Kit caught the outrage in Ty's voice with a small sense of shock. She had hurt him, she realized on an indrawn breath. "It looks as though you're not the only one given to erroneous conclusions," she murmured slowly. She raised her palm to his cheek in a curiously intimate gesture. "I'm sorry."

"Does that mean you don't believe what you said or that you wish you hadn't said it?" he replied, searching her expression with unreadable eyes.

"Both," Kit responded honestly.

He acknowledged her apology, no hint of either relief or satisfaction touching his features. "I'll pick you up at seven." Ty released her and jammed his hands into his pockets.

Kit nodded, more than willing to accept his quick change of subject. The brief pain she had felt at their exchange bothered her more than she was prepared to admit. She watched him stride down her walk and into the night feeling oddly bewildered by what had just happened. For the first time in her adult life, she questioned the wisdom of her actions in agreeing to a date with Harrison Tyler. Was her love of a challenge leading her into disaster? Harrison Tyler represented more than the physical desire she had first recognized and accepted. But how much more?

6

~~~~~~~~~~~

Kit found herself haunted by Ty's commanding presence from the moment she opened her eyes the next morning. Monday was usually a work day, but her date with Tyler meant she went in at two, stayed for a couple of hours and then returned home to prepare for her evening. It should have been a simple procedure. After all, she'd certainly dated before. Yet this time there was a subtle difference, a spring in her step, a certain sparkle about her that was all too apparent to her own jaundiced eye. There was an intoxicating exhilaration coursing through her that was very similar to her feelings at her first parachute jump.

Fear, danger, excitement were all ingredients for a heady wine guaranteed to unleash her reckless spirit and her inhibitions. Yet she knew she couldn't act freely. She had to remember how precarious the present situation was. Much as she wanted to explore the many facets of Harrison Tyler's personality, not to mention the considerable attraction of his body, she had to be careful. She had to give Lydia and Ben their chance without the complication of her relationship with Tyler.

Having made her decision, Kit prepared herself for the hours ahead. She called on the cool discipline she had perfected over the years to subdue the glitter she saw in her exotically made-up eyes. Satisfied with the tranquility of her expression, she slipped her feet into skimpy silver heels and stepped back to survey her sea-green image. From the glossy auburn hair secured in an elegant topknot to the tips of her pearl-tinted toes, she conveyed the serene illusion she intended.

The door chime sounded just as she entered the living room carrying her silver handbag and green and silver lace jacket. She dropped both in the corner of the sofa and went to answer Ty's summons.

"Ty," she murmured in greeting.

Tyler was leaning against the latticework trellis that supported climbing red roses. He pushed himself upright in one fluid motion, his gaze flowing over her with obvious admiration. "You're ready," he commented softly, stepping forward.

Kit retreated a polite pace to let him in, her senses reacting to every part of him. The rich yet discreetly subdued coffee-toned shirt and darker cocoa jacket and the brown, body-hugging herringbone slacks he wore complemented her own outfit. She caught a faint whiff of dampness mingled with the elusive scent of an expensive after-shave as he brushed past her. Kit inhaled carefully, enjoying the combination of fragrance, soap and pure male.

"Would you like a drink before we leave?" she asked, her gaze following his movements with approval. For a big man, he carried himself with surprising grace. Each muscle of his trim body flexed with an effortlessness that was a joy to watch.

"No," he replied, turning to face her. His eyes traveled leisurely over her figure once more. "Do you realize every time I see you I feel like I'm meeting a stranger? You remind me of watching the sun set. No matter how often you witness it, no two are ever the same. Sometimes it's spectacularly beautiful, at others it simply pans gently across the sky."

Bemused by the beauty of his words, Kit stared at him, at a loss. Over the years she'd had her share of compliments, but never one to match this. "Are you always so poetic?" she breathed, more for something to say than any real need to know.

He shook his head as he slowly closed the distance between them. "Oddly enough, I've never felt the urge to be before," he admitted. "But you intrigue me, lady, more every time I see you. You look so cool standing there in that little bit of nothing." His hand hovered a scant inch from her skin as it glided down her body from hip to midthigh. "This slit peeks open every time you walk. If your customers could see you now, you wouldn't have a place big enough to hold them all. No wonder you stick to those jeans and shirts you wear."

Kit dipped her head to stare at her gown. It was an evasive maneuver to escape the yearning in Tyler's black eyes, she acknowledged to herself. Yet it seemed to look natural enough to fool Ty. "Actually, this is one of my more conservative dresses," she murmured, knowing only the most liberal-minded would agree with her. Although the basic off-the-shoulder style was modestly cut, the clingy material coupled with the side slash in the narrow skirt had raised more than one eyebrow.

She shifted restlessly, unwilling to admit how much Ty's proximity bothered her. She was determined to keep their relationship low-key rather than giving in to his subtle persuasion. "Shall we go?" she asked, lifting her deliberately expressionless eyes to his.

Tyler stared at her, the ebony desire in his gaze pouring over her. "You're fighting me. Why?" he demanded in a tone that commanded an answer.

Unsurprised by his bluntness, Kit replied with equal candor, "Because of Lydia. She needs both of us. Right now you and Emily are on one side and I'm on the other. Until Lydia can accept the fact that we all want to help her, we don't dare risk more than this."

One black brow rose sharply in astonishment. "Are you saying that if you and I do more than speak to each other, she's going to think we're ganging up on her?"

Kit nodded. "She's confused, angry and hurt. She's in no mood to be reasonable, especially since Emily has sent for her big gun—you."

"You're crazy," Ty stated flatly, his hands coming up to grasp her shoulders. He glared at her, making no effort to hide his irritation. "You're beginning to sound like my mixed-up niece."

"Good. It shows I'm reading her right," Kit drawled, risking a small smile. "Now shall we go? Frankly, I'm starved. I missed lunch."

Tyler eyed her in frustration. "I'll accept your reasoning for now, but believe me, it won't end here."

With that promise ringing in her ears, Kit half-expected Tyler to continue his provocative maneuvering over dinner. But, surprisingly, he did just the opposite. Her every comfort was attended to with so little fuss she was barely aware of how completely he took care of her. His conversation piqued her interest and fired her imagination. They wined and dined by candlelight, but Kit saw little of the elegant surroundings beyond the intimate setting created just for them.

"That was delicious," she sighed, relaxing in her chair. The waiter had just departed after bringing their coffee. "Now tell me how things went with Lydia."

Ty grimaced at the intrusion of the very subject he preferred to forget, for the moment, anyway. But seeing the determination in Kit's eyes, he knew it was useless to continue postponing the discussion any longer. "Right now we're in a truce, with me being the bad guy. Emily's annoyed because I refused to back her up over her ban on you. Lydia is angry because I spoke to you in the first place. Emily thinks Lydia's working on turning herself into a modern-day version of a B-girl. Lydia's sure my sister's ideas are first cousin to a dinosaur's," he explained tersely, disgust evident in every syllable. "If this is what a real father goes through, I hope I'm sterile."

Kit tried and failed to stifle her laughter at his last

comment. "Tyler," she teased, her eyes filling with tears of amusement, "you're a bachelor, remember."

"Oh, I remember, all right. It's just too bad the rest of you don't remember," he pointed out dryly. "And you quit laughing. This situation is partly your fault, you know. If you'd been the person you were supposed to be, I could have disposed of at least one problem."

"Or traded it for another," Kit shot back between chuckles, for once not hearing an insult about her work in Ty's banter. "Think how much fun you would have had hunting Lydia when she took off."

Ty's expression was clouded and his words were grave. He reached across the table to take Kit's hand in his. "Have I told you how glad I am Lydia found you? She could have been in real trouble if she had gotten friendly with someone less honest."

Warmed by his praise, Kit allowed her fingers to lie in the warm cradle of his palm. A fleeting twinge of conscience over Ben prodded her. "No one's perfectly honest," she murmured, driven to issue a faint warning.

"Perhaps, but I haven't heard any lies from you. So I think my description stands." His grasp tightened on her slender hand. "Are you ready to leave?"

Kit glanced at the delicate silver and diamond watch encircling her wrist. Her eyes widened slightly on seeing how quickly the hours had flown. "It is getting late," she agreed. She'd automatically adjusted herself to the average person's conception of time rather than her own unusual schedule.

"Would you like to stop by Mallory's before we go home?" he asked, cupping her elbow with a light touch. "Lydia has been very vocal about your habits and the club," he elaborated, noticing her surprised expression.

"Okay," she agreed easily.

"This is certainly a change from Saturday night," Ty remarked, his gaze roaming curiously over the quiet crowd. Easy-listening music, punctuated by an occasional upbeat melody, flowed from the old-fashioned jukebox to the left of the vacant bandstand.

"Weeknights like this are for unwinding after a rough day on the job. We try to create an atmosphere of relaxation rather than stimulation," Kit commented, her practiced eye noting the few vacant tables. It was definitely going to be a profitable evening. Her survey ended at the bar with a glance at Ben, who stood quietly at one end. On impulse, she raised her hand to signal him to join them.

"Problem?" Ty asked, one brow lifting in curiosity.

Kit smiled at him reassuringly. "I have someone I'd like you to meet." She turned her head as Ben reached them and made the introductions. "Ben is my cousin as well as being one of the best bartenders around," she added, giving every appearance of merely making idle conversation. In truth, she had a very definite purpose in mind. And with Ty in his present receptive mood, she just might make some progress.

Ben took a seat, dividing his attention carefully between Kit and her companion. "I didn't expect to see you here tonight, boss," he observed after a brief pause.

"Ty suggested we stop by," she explained composedly. "How did your exam go today?"

Ben shrugged, his expression reflecting his puzzlement at her behavior. "I did well, I think."

"Exam?" Ty repeated, entering the conversation for the first time.

Kit flashed him a faint smile. "Ben's studying business administration at Florida Atlantic University. He's only got one more year to go before he gets his degree."

Ben shifted uncomfortably in his chair, clearly embarrassed at the undisguised pride in Kit's voice.

"So you're working here nights and going to school days?" Ty deduced correctly. "That's a tough schedule."

Ben grinned cheerfully. "At first it was murder," he admitted. "But I'm more used to it now and Kit helps a lot by keeping my schedule flexible."

Ty's eyes narrowed thoughtfully at the mention of Kit. Something bothered him about these two. There was a faint hint of tension in the young man, a query in his eyes that Ty found hard to understand. And Kit? He studied her features, searching for a clue to what he sensed but couldn't identify. There was none. She held his gaze without evasion, her expression calm. One russet brow winged upward, questioning his probing. Ty shook his head, slightly annoyed at his cynicism. The woman was honest, he reminded himself, and he was damned tired of his constant need to find flaws in her that simply didn't exist.

"What are you going to do after you graduate?" he asked politely, attempting to cover his blatant scrutiny.

"He's going to take over managing this place for me," Kit answered, knowing Ben would not confide the plans they were making.

Astonished at her unexpected announcement, Ty stared first at one, then the other. "I hadn't realized a bar this size would need you both."

Kit picked up her drink and sipped delicately. "It doesn't. I've been thinking about opening another Mallory's farther up the coast," she explained seriously. "So far the locations I've seen haven't been quite what I have in mind."

Ty seemed intrigued, while Ben appeared confused by the lengthy and uncharacteristically revealing nature of her comments. Kit suppressed a smile at each predictable reaction. Carefully, without appearing to put too much emphasis on Ben's future, she outlined her ideas for expansion and her reasons.

As she had expected, both men became involved in the discussion, hesitantly at first, then, when they were more comfortable with each other, with more freedom. Gradually, satisfied with her strategy, Kit withdrew, leaving them to it.

This was exactly what she had hoped to achieve. Ty might not know it yet, but he was talking to and liking his future nephew. While Ben, in spite of the prejudicial remarks he had heard from Lydia, was finding out more about Harrison Tyler. Tonight might not put them one step closer to a solution, but it might give them a little better understanding of each other. An understanding that could be very important when Tyler found out Ben wanted to marry Lydia.

"I like your cousin," Tyler commented quietly as he parked his car beside Kit's Cougar.

Kit turned her head to examine his strong features, revealed in the light from the lantern outside her door. "I'm glad. He's all the family I've got left," she admitted, giving him another piece of the puzzle, even if he didn't know it yet. "In spite of the differences in our ages we're very close. Although that doesn't seem to stop him from refusing my help with his expenses."

"You wouldn't really respect him if he did," he pointed out. He lifted a hand to her lace-covered shoulder. "And he sure wouldn't respect himself."

Kit nodded, one part of her hearing and agreeing with his words while the other more earthy side was responding to his touch. "I've enjoyed tonight," she murmured softly.

"I have too," he replied in an equally hushed tone. "Could we repeat it again tomorrow or would that cause problems for you at the bar?"

Kit hesitated; with Ty, she had to consider the consequences.

"You're not still worrying about Lydia finding us together, are you? I thought you had changed your mind about that when you wanted to stop at the tavern. She was more likely to see us there than anywhere," he observed, searching her face for an answer to her silence.

"Being seen out occasionally is explainable. Lydia

knows I sympathize with her and she trusts me. But she won't, if she thinks we're involved."

"Does 'involved' mean dining out, or sleeping together? Last night you accused me of wanting any available woman. Surely you know it's you I'm interested in—not just the shape of you?" he demanded.

Kit stiffened at his blunt question. "I didn't say that, but since you brought it up, I'll admit it has crossed my mind. And yours, too, considering the signals you've been sending out." She lifted her fingers to touch his hand, stopping the slow, concentric circles he had been drawing on her shoulder. "You stroke me at every opportunity. You look at me as though I were the main course in some exotic restaurant. Tell me you don't want more than my time."

"More honesty," he rasped, his hand slipping to the vulnerable nape of her neck. "Woman, don't you know anything about finesse?"

"I know more than you think," Kit whispered, feeling him shift closer. Her senses were responding more vividly to him with each inch he stole nearer. She concentrated every ounce of discipline she possessed on resisting his allure. "I know you're staying with Emily. I know that if we spent the night together both your sister and Lydia would know. Emily would have one more reason to dislike me and Lydia would feel betrayed."

"Be quiet, Kit," Ty growled, his lips covering hers in a swift, hungry demand. His mouth devoured hers. Power flowed into him, sending tentacles of heat through his body. He pressed closer to the soft yet strong feminine curves he held. "A taste is not enough," he groaned, drawing back. Excitement such as he had never known with another woman burned within him.

"That's all, Ty," Kit gasped, drawing in a much-needed breath of air. She stared at him, seeing the desire that dilated his pupils. "I only have a few self-made rules in my life and you're trying to make me bend two of them."

"The only thing I'm trying to do is make love to you," he ground out, frustration evident in his expression. "I want you and I think you want me. This is something between us; it has nothing to do with Lydia. If I stayed the night with you, no one would know."

"No one stays with me," Kit replied, leaning back so that her neck was at a more comfortable angle. She breathed a carefully concealed sigh of relief as she watched the passion fade in his eyes.

Ty studied her, a perplexed frown chasing the annoyance from his face. "You're not trying to tell me you're a virgin, are you?"

Kit chuckled, genuinely amused at the combination of horror and skepticism in his expression. "No, I just meant exactly what I said. No man shares my bed."

"Ever?" he clarified slowly.

"Ever," she answered quietly, all trace of levity gone. She gestured toward her town house. "That's my retreat. I spend most of my waking hours surrounded by friends and strangers. This is the only place where I can be totally me." She glanced back at him. "So you see, even if Lydia weren't in the picture, we'd still have a problem with you staying at Emily's."

Ty looked at her intently, trying to understand her. For every question she answered, she left two untouched. She fit no mold he recognized and yet she drew him to her. Damn that madonna expression of hers. She used it like a shield to hide her needs and desires. And how could a man fight that? He wanted— in fact, he was beginning to think he *needed*—her, and all on the strength of a few days' acquaintance. But did she want him? Although she admitted the attraction was there, she continued to resist him.

"All right, we'll play it your way," he agreed finally. "You set the pace, as long as you don't refuse to see me."

Unprepared for the scope of his capitulation, Kit found herself momentarily at a loss. If he only knew it, he'd just outmaneuvered her. She had really thought he'd be angry enough to retract his invitation. "A compromise," she clarified carefully.

He nodded. "Dinner tommorrow night and my promise to let you make the rules."

Put like that, what choice did she have? "At seven again?" she asked in tacit agreement.

"Seven," he repeated firmly before withdrawing his hand from her neck. He slid back to his side of the car in one quick movement, opened his door and got out.

A moment later, Kit watched him stride down her walk toward his car. Her fingers were still tingling from the firm handshake he had given her in lieu of a good-night kiss.

"Smart move," she muttered as her eyes followed his retreating taillights. Instead of testing her with the smallest of caresses, he had given her exactly what she'd asked for. She should have been relieved, but she wasn't. She was distinctly uneasy, wondering why he was being so agreeable.

7

Kit's uneasiness escalated to new heights during their date the following evening. In spite of the daring gold-shot purple silk dress she wore and the intimate setting of one of Palm Beach's most popular restaurants, Tyler had treated her with all the courtesy and respect he would show a maiden aunt. There were no telling little gestures, no subtle innuendos designed to express his desire.

There was, however, lively conversation between them, ranging from politics to their favorite relaxations. She jogged, he swam laps. She liked animals, he'd never had a pet. She was a Democrat, he was a Republican. She enjoyed risks, he preferred a sure thing. For every issue, he stood on one side and she on the other. Yet one fact still remained clear in Kit's mind: Tyler affected her as no other man ever had.

She closed her door slowly after having once again watched him walk away with only a platonic good-bye. "Shadow, my friend, that man is up to something. I can feel it in my bones," she confided. She frowned thoughtfully into space, considering the problem. On the surface, Ty appeared to have accepted her rejection without the slightest show of reluctance. Yet she was unable to shake the feeling that he was playing some deep game with her. But where were the signs, the clues to his dual role? She'd tried all evening to catch him in some slip and had failed to do so.

"It's just too pat," she mumbled, padding toward her softly lit bedroom. Her water bed dominated one wall facing a floor to ceiling section of sliding-glass partitions overlooking the moon-lit, man-made lake.

Her eyes stared at the wide, silver-washed picture before her. He had called her honest and she was. And because of her honesty, she would not allow a relationship to develop between them until he knew the whole story about Ben and Lydia. Much as she wanted him, much as she wanted to tell him the truth, she could not. It was neither her story nor her right. She would sacrifice the pleasure that could be hers so Ty would be free from the bonds of intimacy when the time came for him to choose what he wanted to believe.

"At least he'll be gone until next Monday," she muttered, slipping out of her dress. "Hopefully, out of sight, out of mind."

Kit found the old cliche wasn't true in her case. Oddly, considering how little time she and Tyler had actually spent together, reminders of his presence were everywhere. It started the very next morning with an unexpected visit from Lydia.

"You did say I could stop by," Lydia explained hesitantly as she stood awkwardly at Kit's door.

Kit ran her fingers through her tangled hair in an attempt to smooth it back from her face. After the restless night she'd had, the last thing she needed was Lydia dropping her problems in her lap. Her mind blanked out for a moment as she focused on the cheerfully smiling girl before her. Happy? Lydia?

"You'd better come in," she sighed, stepping aside to let her by. "Have a seat in the living room while I get my clothes on, then I'll make us some coffee." Once in her bathroom, Kit tossed aside her kimono and stepped into the shower. Moments later, dressed in snug-fitting jeans and a peppermint-striped halter and with her hair braided neatly, she made her way to the kitchen.

The smell of fresh-brewed coffee greeted her even before the sound of Lydia's good-humored humming. Puzzled at the girl's high spirits, Kit entered the sunny room.

"Now this is what I call service," she teased, noting Lydia's earnest expression.

Lydia smiled shyly, her eyes showing her pleasure at Kit's reaction. "I woke you up," she explained apologetically. "I really thought you'd be awake since Uncle Ty said you'd gotten in early last night."

Amazed at Lydia's statement as well as her calm acceptance, Kit paused before asking carefully, "You're not upset?"

"Not now," Lydia admitted readily. She turned and

reached into the cabinet behind her to extract a pair of handleless mugs. She filled both and then handed one to Kit. "I was really angry when I found out you and my uncle were dating." She shifted uncomfortably, evading Kit's eyes.

Understanding how difficult it was for Lydia to explain her feelings, Kit gestured toward the small kitchen table. "Let's sit down while you tell me about it," she suggested casually, taking a seat.

Lydia nodded and quickly followed suit. She sat silently for a moment, nervously running her finger over the smooth rim of her mug. "Uncle Ty said you talked about me," she mumbled. She raised her chin, staring worriedly at Kit. "Does he know about Ben and me?"

Kit shook her head, her gaze holding the younger woman's steadily. "You know me better than that. Even though I think you should have told your mother and your uncle the truth, I understand why you didn't."

Lydia brightened at the sympathy in Kit's voice. "At least we're safe."

"No, you're not," Kit warned swiftly. "Tyler is no fool, and from what you've told me, neither is your mother. It won't take long for them to wonder why you're still coming to the bar if you aren't being served or allowed in the main lounge. Ty's met Ben, Lydia."

"I can't tell them, you know that. Mom'll start crying and threatening to send me off to that girl's school upstate. I'll never see Ben again," she wailed dramatically.

Kit clamped her teeth shut against the oath aching

for expression. How foolish to threaten the girl with the I'll-send-you-away routine. In three weeks time Lydia would be eighteen and what was her family planning to do then? Lock her up?

"Nobody's sending you anywhere," she replied firmly. "Your mother was naturally upset. What do you expect from the poor woman?"

"Not you, too?" Lydia gasped, her eyes flashing defiantly. "I thought you were on my side."

"Only as long as you behave like an adult instead of a budding dramatic actress." Kit lifted her cup to her lips and took a small sip of the fragrant brew. She eyed Lydia sternly. "Remember, I'm not your family. I don't have to care about you and I don't need or want your scenes." She placed her mug on the table with careful precision. "I can be a good friend, but I also can be a very nasty foe. It's up to you."

Kit sat back to await the results of her calculated shock treatment. Lydia was well on her way to playing all of them against the others, a situation that would do nothing to alleviate her problems and a great deal to complicate everything.

Lydia stared at her, her eyes wide with amazement. Her pretty features betrayed her dismay. "You wouldn't," she breathed, aghast.

Kit didn't answer her. She sat still, her gaze fixed on Lydia's face. Much as she wanted to comfort Lydia, to promise her everything would be all right, she didn't dare. Lydia had to take responsibility for her own life. Slowly the younger woman seemed to crumple in her chair before Kit's unrelenting appraisal.

"What should I do?" she whispered.

"You tell me," Kit replied.

Lydia gulped audibly. "You want me to tell them about Ben and me."

Kit nodded. "It's only fair, Lydia. Ben deserves more from you than hiding out from your family. It's bad enough you lied to begin with," she pointed out in a slightly softer tone.

"What if they won't let me see him?"

"I don't think that'll happen, not if you explain everything."

Lydia pushed back her chair and got to her feet. She paced over to the glass doors opening onto Kit's small patio. "I don't know if I can do it. Since Uncle Ty talked to Mom about you, she's been so nice. It's almost like it was before Dad left." Lydia swung around, tears brimming in her eyes. "It will all be ruined if I tell them I want to get married. They're going to say I'm too young. Ben can't support me and I won't go to college." She wiped the moisture from her cheeks with an impatient hand.

Kit rose to go to her. She paused a step away, her eyes gentle with sympathy. "You may be right in all you say. But that's not the point. You have to handle yourself as the adult you want to be. You can't hide what you feel; you can't expect Ben to, either. If what you two share is real, it will survive whatever you both ask of it."

Lydia's lips quivered but her gaze remained fixed on Kit's face. "I really have to, don't I?"

"Yes."

Kit's agreement acted as a spring, sending Lydia straight into Kit's arms.

"I'll do it, I promise, but not today," she sobbed, burying her face in Kit's shoulder.

Kit held her lightly, feeling the tremors shaking Lydia's petite frame. "The longer you wait, the harder it's going to be," she warned softly.

Lydia nodded, her face muffled. "I know." She pushed herself reluctantly away from Kit's body. Sniffing, she dried her eyes on the tail end of her yellow T-shirt. "I better go or I'll be late to school."

Kit followed her to the door. "Call me if you need me," she reminded her as Lydia paused on the porch.

Lydia looked somehow more mature than when she arrived. "I will," she promised with careful dignity. "I'll let you know when I've done it, too." With a lift of her hand, she turned and walked toward her car.

Kit stood in her doorway for a long moment after Lydia had gone. It was becoming something of a habit for her to watch Lydia and her uncle stride down her walk. She should be feeling crowded by this sudden intrusion into her sanctuary, she realized, yet she wasn't. Somehow it seemed natural to be offering her support and the quiet of her home to Tyler and his niece. Kit closed her door and began her interrupted daily routine.

Lydia's departure brought a return of the even tempo of Kit's life. There were no more scenes from either Lydia or Ty. Ben was more relaxed then usual and far less worried about Lydia, he confided three evenings later as they were closing the pub.

"Has Lydia told her mother about you two yet?" she asked, pausing in the middle of counting the cash for the next day into the register drawer.

Ben shook his head as he leaned against the edge of her desk, watching her. "She says she will soon. She invited me to her mother's for supper this Sunday."

Kit's eyebrows rose in surprise at his unexpected announcement. "And?" she prompted when he made no effort to explain his startling news.

"I'm going," he grinned, suddenly looking years younger. "According to Lydia, she overheard her uncle telling her mom to ease up on her. It seems it was his suggestion that she invite one or both of us over."

Kit frowned thoughtfully, trying to imagine the Emily she knew only at second hand agreeing with her strong-minded brother. "I wonder why she's going along with the idea," she mused aloud.

Ben shrugged. "That bothered me too at first," he admitted slowly. He studied the tips of his well-worn shoes for a moment before lifting his gaze to Kit's face. "But the fact is I can't afford to care why Emily Nelson is extending the invitation. I need to meet her and she needs to meet me. And if I'm very careful to mind my manners, she just might rethink some of her ideas about you and me." He paused, then added, "At least it's worth a try."

"I wonder why she didn't wait until after Tyler gets back on Monday? Considering how quick she was to call him for help, you'd think she'd welcome his support in this."

"Maybe," Ben agreed cautiously, struck by her reasoning. "I'm still going."

Kit agreed. In his place she'd do the same, regardless of the risks. "Just be careful that you uphold the family honor," she told him with teasing seriousness. She placed the cash tray in the safe and closed it with a click of the tumblers. "I'm beat. Let's go home." She stretched her body, easing the weariness of her cramped muscles. "One more day and we get a rest," she groaned.

Puzzled by her uncharacteristic display of fatigue, Ben studied her closely. "Are you catching a cold or something?" he asked.

Kit shot him a swift glance, reading the concern in his eyes. "You know I never get sick," she chided, wishing she hadn't mentioned her tiredness. She was well aware of how odd it was for her to feel eager for a day off, much less to admit she wanted one. Except for her quarterly junkets, when she indulged her need for adventure, she always gave every appearance of being perfectly content with her life and the demands it made on her.

Ben touched her arm gently. "Is there a problem? You know I'm here if you need me."

Kit smiled, warmed by his caring, although she had no intention of sharing the causes of the washed-out look she saw in her mirror every morning. It was annoying enough to know it was there without trying to explain why she was affected by a man she barely knew. "Nothing's wrong. I've just been having a few late nights and I need to catch up on my sleep."

Ben opened his mouth to voice his opinion of the lie

they both recognized, then changed his mind. "We'd better get going then," he suggested instead.

Kit grimaced as she surveyed her reflection the next morning. Another night with only fitful periods of sleep had painted deep lavender shadows beneath her eyes. Even her hair, which was usually alive with color and bounce, lay in limp strands against her shoulders.

"What are you doing to me, Harrison Tyler?" she demanded, glaring at her pale image. "Taking you into my bed would have been easier than this." She collected a swath of her hair in one hand and drew it across her shoulder. The long auburn tresses flowed over her naked body to brush her skin with tantalizing softness. The whisper touch coupled with the unappeased desire torturing her body made a mockery of her control. "Blast you, Tyler, get out of my head!" she swore, whirling away from the hungry woman staring back at her. "I won't give in to this until only the truth lies between us. Then I don't think I'll wait to be asked."

Considering her frame of mind, Kit was relieved at how quickly the day flew by. If a little voice kept reminding her that there were only twenty-four hours left until Tyler returned, she did her best to ignore it and concentrate on the matters at hand. In no time at all, Kit was back in her apartment preparing for bed once more. Only this time she was asleep from the moment she snuggled into her pillow. Her nocturnal restlessness had finally taken its toll. She awoke late Sunday and spent the day attending to the many household chores she neglected during the week.

Inevitably, Monday arrived, and with it a case of nerves. Every time the phone rang she jumped, expecting it to be Ty. She went to the tavern without having heard from him.

The only good point of the evening was Ben's report on the dinner with Lydia and her mother. It had gone far better than he had expected. While Emily wasn't reconciled to Lydia's presence at the bar, at least she wasn't openly hostile toward Ben.

By closing time Kit was fighting an overwhelming sense of disappointment. She'd been so sure Ty would come. With Shadow by her side, she got into her car for the long drive home. "I can't believe he didn't stop by," she told the dog, her eyes fixed on the almost empty road ahead. "I can't believe how much I counted on seeing him." Her second comment contained an added depth of wonder that her first statement lacked. "He's not supposed to mean this much to me."

Shadow whined sympathetically as he thrust his sleek head into her lap. Kit's hand dropped to the satiny fur, petting the black pelt with long strokes.

"I hope Lydia tells them soon," she murmured feelingly. "At least everything will be out in the open. Then if Tyler doesn't want me, I'll be able to get him out of my system." She paused, contemplating that prospect. She had a sinking feeling it was going to be easier said than done, and a lot more painful.

Kit turned down her street, her eyes widening at the presence of Tyler's LTD parked in her visitor's slot. Her fingers tightened on the steering wheel as she guided her Cougar to a stop beside his sedan. He got out of his vehicle at the same moment she did.

"Hello, Kit." His quiet greeting floated on the air between them.

"Tyler," she replied with an equal lack of emphasis. A brief flash of two duelists poised with swords raised appeared before her mind's eye as she stared at her caller. "I didn't expect you this late."

"I almost didn't come."

Wary, yet with her senses tingling with life, she moved toward him, Shadow keeping pace with her. Tyler fell into step beside her as she came level with him. Unlocking her front door, she led the way inside.

"Would you like a drink?" she asked, turning to face him in the softly lit foyer.

His lips curved into what could have been a smile at her commonplace question if it wasn't for the gleam of mockery in his eyes. "No, I didn't come here for that," he responded in a rich velvet purr.

Kit's eyes sparked with burnished gold at his expression as well as his words. Her week had been anything but pleasant and it was all his fault. "Why *are* you here?" she demanded, deliberately ignoring the signals he was sending out.

Something hardened in Ty's eyes at her blunt question. He closed the distance between them, his onyx gaze fixed commandingly on her. "I came for you," he announced with such deadly calm it took a full minute for his pronouncement to take effect.

When it did, Kit's whole body tautened with anger and a strange exhilaration. Here at last was the target on which she could vent her frustration and her temper. "What makes you think you can have me?" she shot back, not in the least intimidated by the fact that he was looming over her like some great, angry being.

"Because you look as bad as I do." He slipped the perceptive thrust in with all the delicacy of a master swordsman. He lifted his hand to lightly touch the lingering shadows that marred her champagne-colored skin. "I've ached every night to hold you. I haven't slept worth a damn since I left," he growled roughly, dropping his hand to his side once again.

Sheer shock at his admission in the face of his masculine arrogance swept away the words she'd intended to hurl at him. For the first time since he'd arrived, she really studied him. New lines had been etched on his face, accentuating faint hollows that hadn't been there the week before. There was a barely detectable aura of exhaustion surrounding him that was new yet strangely appealing.

"Has it really been bad for you?" she asked slowly, unable to suppress the satisfaction she felt at knowing he'd been as affected by her as she was by him. She longed to reach out to touch him yet she sensed that if she did the restraint they both were exercising would dissolve. She wasn't ready for that and she had a feeling he wasn't either.

"It's been hell," he answered after a short pause. He inhaled slowly, filling his lungs with her elusive scent. Night after night her fragrance had haunted him; enticing, challenging, it held all the subtlety that was uniquely Kit. And now she stood before him, her eyes alive with emotions she rarely showed. Her madonna expression was just as serene and tranquil as he remembered, denying everything the mirrors of her soul betrayed. Heat filled his body, bringing life to a desire that was almost painful in its intensity. God, how he wanted this woman.

Kit felt passion licking up like a flame to dry tinder to engulf them. Neither of them had moved, but it was as though the inches separating them were slowly diminishing. She stared into his eyes, her fingers curling into her palms in an effort to keep from reaching out to him.

"I've rented a hotel suite," he ground out, his voice sounding harsh in the charged atmosphere holding them captive.

"There's still Lydia," Kit parried, somehow unsurprised at his words.

"Must it be one or the other?" he demanded. He leaned imperceptibly closer, his gaze commanding her to tell him nothing could stand between them.

Pinned by the full force of his will and his need, Kit swayed. How easy it would be to give in. How she wanted to seize this moment and the passion he offered her. But the truth she hid rose like a barrier between them. She couldn't become truly involved with this man until he knew everything. The betrayal he would feel after their intimacy would hurt them both and any chance they had for a future.

"I can't," she groaned with a pained whimper. She closed her eyes for a moment to shut out the disbelief reflected in Ty's strained eyes. Her lashes lifted almost immediately as she faced him bravely. "When this is

119

over, ask me again." It was a plea—the only one she would make.

"Why?" he grated. His shock at her answer was clear for her to see. He lifted his hands as though he would grab her and force the words he sought from her lips. A heartbeat later he dropped them slackly to his sides, reading her refusal in her eyes.

"I can't tell you. God help me, I wish I could."

He stared at her, hearing the pain, the need that she made no effort to hide. Then he nodded abruptly, knowing he had to accept her verdict without understanding it. "I want to kiss you."

"Please don't," she said, swiftly retreating from his request as she hadn't from his anger. "Just go before I forget my reasons for putting us through this." She wrapped her arms around her waist to ward off the encroaching chill of separation.

"Are you sure?" He had to try to change her mind one last time.

"I am." Her eyes begged him to leave.

He turned toward the door, his back to her. "How will I know when it's time?"

Kit's eyes filled at the dark yearning in his voice. "You'll know. Believe me, you'll know."

8

Tyler," Kit gasped in surprise, staring at the man leaning lazily against her doorjamb. "What are you doing here?" Her eyes drank in the sight of him before she had a chance to gather her composure. Why was he here now? Last night had been a painful ordeal. Must she go through it again?

"I came to take you to breakfast," he drawled, clearly enjoying the sight of her confusion. His gaze flowed over her like ebony velvet, deep, compelling and infinitely soothing. The desire that had burned so brightly the evening before was swathed in a warm blanket of friendliness.

Kit registered the change with wariness. "I thought we settled this last night," she said, remaining firmly in place, her body blocking his entrance to her town house. She was all too conscious of how little her gold satin kimono covered. Being awakened out of a sound sleep by the ringing of her doorbell was definitely not conducive to her retaining her poise.

Tyler smiled, a slow widening of his lips guaranteed to raise any normal woman's blood pressure a few degrees. He lifted his hands, palms up. "I offered you a meal, not me," he chided gently.

For the first time since she had left adolescence behind, Kit blushed, a fine golden rose suffusing her cheeks. "I'm aware of that," she shot back, wishing she had the nerve to shut the door between them. Or to brush her hair at least, she amended, as a tangle of auburn strands caught by the midmorning breeze fell across her forehead.

Ty reached up as if to brush the feathery whisps back, then stopped. For a split second his fingers hovered a breath away from the satin smoothness of her skin. "I promised myself I wouldn't touch you," he mused softly, his eyes fathoms deep with emotions Kit barely recognized. "I wanted us to get to know each other. I think you're afraid to trust me because of Lydia." His lips twisted ruefully. "And after my initial reaction, I don't blame you."

Cautiously, Kit studied him, reading nothing but sincerity in his expression. "We tried this before," she pointed out. "What makes you think this time will be any different?"

His gaze never faltered in the face of her skepticism. "Because I'm not asking or expecting one thing more than you're prepared to give," he replied honestly. "I'm willing to settle for simply being with you if that's all you want."

Kit nibbled at her lower lip, considering. On the one hand, she was unable to deny the appeal of sharing her day with Ty. Yet she wondered if her control would hold. Just standing in front of him was heating her body.

"Okay," she murmured at last. Her resistance was overshadowed by the compulsion she felt to be near him. "Let me change my clothes." She paused, eyeing him curiously. "Where are we going?"

Ty chuckled at her expectant expression. "Lydia tells me you're a great windsurfer. I've always wanted to learn. Are you willing to teach me?"

Pleased and reassured by the innocent nature of his plans, Kit's sherry eyes lit with enthusiasm. "Have you ever surfed?"

"A long time ago," he admitted wryly. "Is that a requirement?"

Kit shook her head, further tangling her sleep-mussed hair. "No, but it helps." She gestured toward her kitchen. "It's a little on the cool side today so we'd better take a couple of wet-suit jackets. There's a closet beside the pantry with my swim gear. There should be a jacket in there to fit you. Mine's the yellow one." She headed toward her bedroom. "You can make some coffee if you want it," she added over her shoulder.

Slipping out of her simple covering, Kit swiftly donned a brief turquoise French-cut one-piece suit. The thin material molded her curves with the front and rear panels laced together at the sides from the bodice to the leg openings. Golden skin gleamed like silk between the crisscrossed strips accentuating her long, curvy body. A hip-length coverup in a matching fabric draped gracefully over one arm to fasten toga-style at her shoulder with a small bow.

She brushed and tightly braided her hair before winding it into a coronet around her head. This was one time her plait got in the way of the quick action required for windsurfing.

Ty was waiting for her when she reentered the living room. He handed her a steaming mug of coffee. "Since I got you out of bed before you could have your first cup, I fixed this for you," he explained easily, his fingers brushing hers lightly as he withdrew his hand.

Kit cupped the warm china in her palms, vividly aware of the brief contact. Her lashes dropped in a defensive gesture, shielding her involuntary reaction. "Thanks," she breathed softly in a tone a shade huskier than normal. She sipped the dark liquid while mentally shoring up her wavering control. If Ty could stand there looking totally relaxed and unaffected, then so could she. There was a moment of silence as they shared their stand-up breakfast.

Ty drained his cup. "I filled the Thermos I found in the closet with coffee." He indicated the corner of the sofa beside which lay a small pile of equipment. "Two wet-suit tops, two beach towels." He pinned her with a dark probing look. "I know I haven't the right to ask this, but why do you have two of everything and especially something large enough to fit me?"

"My stepfather," she responded candidly. "And you're right, you really shouldn't have asked." Her lips curved slightly. "But I suppose I should be grateful you did, instead of jumping to conclusions again."

Tyler grimaced at her reminder. "Let's go before you change your mind about going out with me," he said, plucking her empty mug from her hands. "Your car or mine?"

"Mine, because I've got the racks to carry our boards."

"I knew we forgot something. Where do we rent the surfers?"

Kit dangled a small gold key in front of him. "We don't. We walk out to the storage room in the patio and pick them up."

Ty pulled the key from her grasp. "I'll do that. You get this stuff." He grinned at her indignation at being relegated to the easier task. "Don't worry, I'm not putting you in your place," he teased, openly enjoying her spurt of temper. "You're going to be the one to mount those things on your car. In my day we only stuck the board through an open window onto the backseat."

Laughing at his nonsensical explanation, Kit bent over to collect their gear. "I think I'm being snowed, but in the interest of peace, I'll let you get away with it this time," she decided, eyeing him with mock sternness. "Let's hit the beach."

Two hours later, Kit called a laughing halt to Ty's initiation into one of her favorite sports. "I think you cheated," she accused as he gracefully dismounted from his board beside her. She stood waist deep in the water eyeing his water-slick body with admiration. "You handled that sail like a pro."

Ty shrugged, bracing himself against the ebb and surge of the waves breaking around them. "Pro?" he groaned theatrically. "I took at least five spills before I managed to get that triangular demon to obey me."

"Six," Kit corrected, a wicked gleam in her eye. "But who's counting." She tugged on the contoured fiberglass craft she held steady with one hand. "I'm surfed out. Are you ready to quit?"

"I thought you'd never ask," he agreed, pushing his sail-rigged surfboard toward the deserted beach.

Kit followed him out of the water, dragging her board to rest beside his. Then she dropped down on her spread-out beach towel and leaned back on her elbows to stare out at the sea. From the corner of her eye she saw Ty assume a similar position a fingertip's length away.

"Tell me about your life," he invited, keeping his eyes fixed firmly on the horizon. It was either that or crush her sun-warmed body in his arms and drink his fill of her salt-kissed lips. He flexed his muscles, feeling the tension in each separate ligament, reflecting the control he was exercising.

"There's not much to tell," Kit replied, all too aware of his proximity. Out on the waves it had been so much easier to rechannel her attraction into physical activity. But here, cradled on a natural couch of earth with only the elements to witness her need, she found it hard to remember her resolve.

"I can't get to know you if you won't talk to me," he

reminded her, his voice several notes deeper than it had been. "Tell me more about your mother and your stepfather."

Kit risked a sidelong glance at him through the screen of her lashes. Droplets of water formed crystal prisms over his taut flesh, drawing her eye. The tiny, diamond-clear beads obeyed the laws of gravity by flowing slowly, tantalizingly down his muscled chest to his flat abdomen. There they were absorbed by the black knit waistband of his swimsuit.

Moistening her suddenly dry lips, Kit snatched her thoughts away from the allure of his masculine form. "I met Dan when I was fifteen," she admitted starkly, more interested in breaking the silence than in the telling of her past. "I meant what I said about being a hellraiser."

"You must have liked him right from the beginning," Ty prompted, equally intent on keeping the conversation going.

"Yes, he was an extraordinary man. Generous in spirit as well as in a material sense. He was so good to Mom about her hours and letting her off when I got into trouble at school. After the third time, he stepped in himself. I didn't know it then, but my life changed at that moment. I used to spout the trashiest nonsense— far worse than anything Lydia's said. He'd listen, never saying a word to stop me. Then when I ran down, he'd throw some earth-shattering truth at me in the calmest voice you ever heard." She grinned, remembering how unnerving it had been for her.

"Then what happened?"

"I couldn't answer him because he was right. So right even I had to know it." She turned slightly to face him. "I never saw him angry. For the longest time, I tried to make him lose his temper, but he never did. I think that's what impressed me the most. I couldn't make him retaliate no matter how badly I acted."

"So you learned how to be like him," Ty noted perceptively.

She nodded slowly. "In a way, but not completely. I learned to control my temper; I have an absolutely wicked one when I let go. Also I learned to channel my restlessness into a productive direction."

"Mallory's."

She nodded, by now accustomed to his ability to understand the small nuances that escaped most people. "I never have gotten rid of my risk-taking nature," she admitted, her announcement sounding strangely like a warning. "About every three months I get an urge to try something really wild."

Ty's brows shot up in amazement. "You?" he questioned in disbelief. "You're kidding. I can't imagine you doing anything wilder than maybe windsurfing."

Kit laughed huskily, enjoying his shock at her confession. "Do you know, you're one of the few people who know about my secret life."

Ty's eyes darkened to midnight. "Am I?" he asked, his expression gentling to match the deep throb in his voice. "Tell me about your dangerous other self," he invited softly, edging carefully nearer.

Kit lost herself in his ebony gaze. What had begun

as a defense against Ty's effect on her had backfired. Awareness shimmered around them, entangling her in a net of desire. What an overconfident fool she was to believe she could steal this time with Ty and escape unscathed. She inhaled slowly, striving to ignore his presence.

"I've tried skydiving, amateur drag racing, crossbow hunting and even a short stint of hot-air ballooning," she enumerated absently as she stared into the bottomless depths of his eyes. "Next I plan on trying hydroplaning," she added, using the flimsy words as a barrier against the ever-tightening mesh of Ty's will. "Don't do this," she whispered, unconsciously swaying closer to him. "You promised to help. I can't fight both of us."

"Don't try," he rasped, his fingers sliding lightly up her damp body to rest just under the swell of her breast. "Do you have any idea how intoxicating you are? You sit here like a sea goddess in repose, discussing doing things that most men wouldn't even attempt." His hand splayed across her skin as he drew her still closer. "You're burning me up inside, woman. You intrigue me with your untouchable air, you tantalize me with a body I ache to possess and then confound me with your mind and your need for a challenge. How can I resist you?" he demanded, bending his head to brush her lips with his.

"Try," she pleaded, sipping his warm breath as she would a fine cognac. Her tongue slipped from between her lips to trace the contour of his questing mouth.

Ty sank his teeth tenderly into her bottom lip, suckling erotically on the lush curve. "I don't want to try." He arched against her pliant body, his taut contours telling of his arousal. "I need you, can't you understand? Desire, passion—they're there, too. But I need you, Kit Mallory. Put away your scruples and come to me."

Kit curled her arms about his neck, succumbing to his masculine allure. "There is something about me I want you to know before we share this—"

"I know all I need to know," Ty interrupted swiftly, sensing her capitulation. "Trust me as I trust you."

Caught by the plea in his voice and her own spiraling needs, Kit struggled briefly with her conscience.

"Surrender, Kit," he growled, his lips trailing liquid-fire kisses across her jaw to the sensitive hollow behind her ear. "I've already raised the white flag."

"Ty," she breathed, her resolve dying in the face of the powerful forces binding them together. She turned her head, searching blindly for his lips. Her fingers closed on the hard thrust of his shoulders before sliding up to entwine themselves in his thick hair.

"That's it, hold me, honey," he whispered hoarsely, gathering her tightly against his chest.

The world lurched and swirled for Kit as he rose, somehow cradling her and their towels in his arms. Dazed at the sheer strength required, Kit lay quiescent in his embrace. She stared at the clean profile silhouetted against the cerulean sky with a dawning sense of wonder. Was this protected, cherished feeling what women felt with their chosen mates? For once in her life she wished she were beautiful.

"You're exquisite." He lowered Kit with the towel beneath her in a soft sand clearing rimmed by the tall sea oats. The slender blades provided a delicate, lacy screen, sealing them away from the world as completely as the closing of a bedroom door.

"I want to be," Kit murmured softly, her eyes glowing with passion, desire and longing.

He knelt beside her without ever freeing her from his embrace. "You've haunted my nights for so long." His hands slipped up to the nape of her neck to release the small bow securing her swimsuit.

Kit noticed the slight shaking of his hands and the throb of the pulse at his temple, tiny signs telling of his vulnerability to her. His eyes were warmly intent as he eased the top of her suit down to reveal the full curve of her naked breasts. He drew a deep, unsteady breath as he reached out to gently cup the warm silken softness. He leaned forward, admiration flowing from his touch and his gaze. His lips anointed each peak with the lightest of kisses, bringing a gasp of aching pleasure to Kit's throat.

Kit trembled, the yearning within her twisting higher. "Touch me," she pleaded in a husky throb, arching to meet his mouth as it hovered a breath away.

Ty shook his head, each motion stirring a faint whisper of air across her bare skin. "I want to love you, Kit, slowly and completely. Don't ask me to rush."

His thumbs gently stroked her nipples as Kit responded eagerly to his manipulations and the evocative effect of his words. She looked up at him, her eyes oddly grave. "I want you to love me," she agreed with a velvet throb in her voice. She slid closer to his virile strength, needing the heat of him to surround her. She slipped her arms around his waist and pressed her bare breasts to his muscled chest. He had only to touch her to start this throbbing ache in her loins.

A violent shudder shook him as she writhed beneath him. She pressed kisses along the straight line of his shoulder, her tongue flicking out to tease and taste his flesh. She lifted herself, working her way up his throat to the edge of his jaw. She was so engrossed in her exploration of him and the satisfaction she received at his every response that she scarcely noticed him peeling the suit from her body.

Ty finally tossed away the turquoise wisp, then angled his head to capture Kit's adventurous lips. His tongue invaded her mouth with hot urgency, exploring and playing with her own until they were consumed with mutual hunger. Kit slipped her hands down his back to smooth the black briefs over his hips.

"I'll do it, honey," he said, moving her hands away from his waist. "I want this to last, and when you touch me I go up in smoke." He rose and quickly stripped before her admiring eyes.

Kit feasted on the portrait of golden male before a backdrop of deep verdant grasses, a sunlit sky and the noise of the ocean.

Ty came down on the towel to ease Kit onto her back so that she was lying full-length before him. His fingers traced the curve of her cheek to her temple before he began unpinning her hair. "I want to see it down," he explained, watching her face intently. "I want to see you veiled in it the way nature intended women to be clothed."

Kit smiled slightly at the primitive image he created. "I never would have known you were so basic," she replied with gentle humor, while marveling at the ease she felt in their open-air seclusion. Every part of her was alive to the sensual pleasures his body gave her. Yet there was a special quality in this foreplay that soothed and stimulated at one and the same time.

Ty combed his fingers through her unbound hair, arranging the long, dark strands across her body. Tiny pink buds peeked shyly through the auburn strands while a darker triangle of curls at the juncture of her thighs blended with feathery ends to create an illusion of modesty. He placed a trembling hand on her soft belly and began a slow massaging motion that had Kit arching ardently against his heated touch.

He lowered his head to brush his lips where his hand had been caressing. "You're all woman, Kit Mallory. Soft, warm, strong, passionate."

His tongue darted out to stroke her sensitive flesh and Kit inhaled sharply as her body quivered in response. Leisurely, he nibbled every inch unprotected by her hair. His hands traced lazy, tantalizing patterns on her thighs until Kit felt she would go insane with wanting him.

Each touch was a galvanic shock, each teasing bite fed a fever that generated a molten ache in every limb.

Her breath came in light pants between her parted lips. Moans born of unappeased desire grew in her throat.

Ty raised his head, his expression mirroring his almost savage pleasure in her response. He smiled into her passion-dark eyes before resuming his tormenting loveplay.

Kit bit her lip in frustration at the maddening pace of his teasing arousal. Even in her highly charged state she recognized his tactics. So he would bind her to him with passion, would he? Part of her rejoiced at his obvious need to make her his, yet her strength demanded she also take him as her own. Kit clutched at his shoulders, her nails unconsciously digging into him with the urgency of her need.

Ty laughed deep in his throat and lifted his head to look at her with gleaming black eyes. "That's right. Put your marks on me, my daredevil madonna. I want to look at them later and remember how we were together." He slipped a hand between her thighs.

Kit's lips curved with wicked intent as she felt him reposition himself to accommodate her. With one swift movement, she closed her legs, capturing him in her soft warmth. At the same time, she turned until Ty rolled on his back with her on top. "You took too long," she breathed throatily.

She moved over him, rubbing her breasts against his chest as she made tiny bites on his shoulder. Winding her way down his body, she teased and caressed his male nipples, duplicating the pleasure he had given her. His heartbeat accelerated beneath her palm, telling her of his arousal. His muscles knotted with tension as she moved slowly across his hard stomach. When she sipped at the well of his navel, he arched toward her with a wild groan deep in his throat.

"Enough, woman," he ordered thickly, urging her up. His hands fanned out under her breasts, lifting her into position above him. With a hard-driving thrust he plunged into her, seeking the deepest core of her femininity.

Kit's lashes drifted closed as she savored the primitive sensation of their mating. Head thrown back in passionate abandon, she lost herself in the fiery rhythm he set. His hands were everywhere, stroking, kneading, caressing. Tension mounted within her, filling every particle of her being. Heat flowed through her, fusing her body to the pulsating male creature, driving them toward a burning climax.

Higher, faster, each muscle straining for the peak coming ever closer. Just when Kit was certain she could stand no more, Ty arched up and over in one powerful surge. Tension shattered into tiny splinters. Twin cries of satisfaction rose to the sky as they collapsed in each other's arms. Perspiration from their union shone gold in the sun as they lay entwined. Kit held Ty to her, aware of his every breath.

In the aftermath of their joining, one fact stood clear. She *loved* him, completely and irrevocably. She had never known such fulfillment nor had she ever given so totally of herself. She could not regret this moment, yet she knew the reckoning, when it came, would bring her pain beyond measure. She couldn't imagine Ty understanding her holding back about Ben and Lydia. Nor could she see him forgiving her for this betrayal when she knew what stood between them. He thought her honest. He had even conquered his prejudices about her. He spoke of trust.

Unaccustomed tears gathered in her eyes at the thought of the future. She had dared to risk everything so many times without fear, but she was afraid now.

9

Kit?"

At the sound of Ty's voice, Kit's fingers tightened on the phone receiver. Memories of their passionate afternoon flooded her with a sweet aching warmth. In spite of everything, she couldn't regret their lovemaking. It had been too deep, too intense for wishing away.

"Ty," she breathed huskily in greeting. "Are you calling to tell me I don't get anchovies on my pizza after all?"

He chuckled softly, his amusement wrapping around her like a cozy blanket. "I wish it was that simple," he replied with a groan.

"Problems?" Kit leaned back in her chair and propped her feet up on the corner of her desk. Had it only been five hours since Ty had left her at her town house? It seemed more like days.

"Honey, I won't be coming to the pub tonight. There was a message from Jacksonville waiting for me when I got back. Bob, my second in command, is having trouble with a presentation," he explained, his humor changing to frustrated annoyance. "I'll have to straighten it out from here, otherwise I'll have to fly up to the office."

"Oh," she murmured inadequately. Disappointment welled within her, startling her with its intensity. Without realizing it, she'd been counting on seeing Ty again. What had happened between them had been so new, so strong, she'd needed his presence to reassure her of the passion they'd shared.

"I'm sorry, Kit, more than I can say." His voice deepened with suppressed emotion. "I needed to be with you tonight just so I'll know this afternoon was no dream."

Kit pressed the phone to her ear as though attempting to bring him closer to her. "Me, too," she admitted involuntarily. At another time, with someone else, she would never have been so forthcoming. But with Ty she had no need of secrets or evasions. "Will I see you tomorrow?"

Ty hesitated fractionally before replying. "I don't know, honey. I'll try my best. Are you going to be home?"

Kit nodded, forgetting for a moment that Ty couldn't see her. "Yes," she said when she realised he was still waiting for her answer.

"Good," he murmured, an odd note in his voice. "I'm working on something I may need your help with."

A moment later Kit hung up the phone, wondering at Ty's cryptic words and the hint of satisfaction she had heard in them. What could he possibly require her help with except Lydia? If it was his rebellious niece, then why the mysterious teaser? Why hadn't he just explained?

Shaking her head to clear it of muddled thoughts, Kit frowned at the seascape on her far wall. For every question Ty answered, two seemed to crop up almost immediately to plague her. For someone who preferred emotional order to chaos in her everyday life, she was definitely having no success in dealing with her growing relationship with Ty.

Fleetingly, she wished for a friend to confide in. Just as quickly as the idea was born, she thought of Summer. Now there was the person to ask, she decided. Her expression eased slightly as she reached for the phone. Her fingers curled around the cool plastic of the receiver a split second before she jerked her hand away. She stared at the innocent object with something close to accusation in her eyes.

"Blast that man," she muttered irritably. "Now he's even got me thinking about boring my friend with my love life." She pushed back from her desk to get to her feet. "Stay, Shadow," she ordered, glancing at her canine companion. The dark reproach in his liquid eyes softened the edge of her mood. "I'm only going out to sit with Ben for a while." She knew that although the dog didn't understand every word she said, he recognized Ben's familiar name and lay down once again.

As she entered the lounge she caught Ben's surprised glance. She made her way slowly to the bar and took a seat.

"What's up?" he asked as soon as he'd finished his current drink orders.

Kit shrugged, not about to admit she needed something to take her mind off her ebony-eyed lover. "I'm just restless, I guess," she explained, offering him an excuse she knew he would accept.

Ben grinned, his expression wryly sympathetic. "It's getting toward that time of year," he teased.

Bewildered by his comment, it took Kit a second to realize he was referring to her quarterly junkets. "Three more weeks," she agreed, silently wondering what Ty would be doing then. Would he have forgotten all about her? Or would they still be together?

"Are you all right?"

Ben's worried question pulled Kit from the future back to the present with a jolt. "Of course," she replied automatically, beginning to wish she'd remained in her office after all.

Silently, Ben examined her suddenly guarded face. "Has Lydia's uncle been giving you trouble again?" he probed gently.

Kit's lashes flickered down in a faint gesture of betrayal before she faced his gaze squarely. "Much as I care about you, don't ask me any more," she commanded quietly. Another secret, she reminded herself ruefully. But how could she confide in Ben? If he knew the strain his love for Lydia had placed on her, he would insist on talking to Emily and Ty regardless of the cost to himself or Lydia.

Puzzlement turned to comprehension as he searched her eyes. "He's important."

It was a statement, not a question, and they both knew it. Kit inclined her head, deliberately blanking her expression to hide what had to be concealed. But it was no use. She saw it even before Ben put his conclusions into words.

"You haven't told him about Lydia and me. Knowing you, you're feeling guilty about it." He paused just long enough to be certain no customers were waiting for his attention. "I'm talking to them tomorrow," he decided firmly, determination adding new lines to his features. "We should have explained everything in the beginning. All this sneaking around is a real—"

"Stop it," Kit ordered, interrupting him without compunction. "None of us is sneaking around." Her voice rang with conviction. "Lydia needed you and breathing space. Whatever our personal feelings were then or now, we had to give her that chance. Have you forgotten how close to running away she was? Tell me you don't know the statistics on girls her age with her looks. We'd all be darned lucky if she didn't end up walking the streets just to survive." Suddenly realizing her voice had grown stronger with each word, Kit looked around to see if they were attracting attention. Fortunately, everyone was too involved in having a good time to notice them.

Ben held up one palm in surrender. "Okay, I know you're right," he admitted slowly, his upraised hand lowering to clench in frustration. "But when will this end? And supposing either Lydia's mother or her uncle finds out before we tell them? Can you imagine how we'll look? What about what it'll do to Lydia?"

"Believe me, I've thought about all of this," she sighed wearily, slipping off her perch. "We're running a big risk, but what else can we do?"

Sherry eyes met hazel, understanding and fatalistic acceptance reflected in each. "I'm going back to the office," she stated, her calm public mask firmly in place once more.

"I guess I'll get back to work."

Kit recognized the strength Ben was displaying by putting aside his feelings and doing what was best for the girl he loved. She and Ben were bound together to help Lydia. Yet even if Ben and Lydia were forced apart temporarily, until Lydia came of age, they still had a chance at happiness. But what of her and Ty? Could he forgive her lie of omission when he knew she was fully aware of his concern for his sister and niece? Or would he feel she should've trusted him in spite of everything?

Questions, always unanswerable, plagued her. Only time and, perhaps, a kindly providence held a solution. The dawning of another day brought no change in her feelings or her situation. She was committed now. She regretted the half-truths she'd had to tell Ty, but she would not change them even if she could. If saving Lydia cost her his love, then so be it.

"You sound disgustingly cheerful," Summer teased with a grin as she entered the kitchen unannounced.

Kit whirled around at the sound of her voice, nearly

dropping the mug she held. She had been so engrossed in preparing breakfast for herself and Shadow, that she hadn't heard Summer enter. "You'd think I'd remember to lock my door when I finish my run," she complained jokingly. She waved Summer to a seat at the table. "Of course, if I had a friend who believed in knocking, I wouldn't worry about it."

Summer chuckled unrepentently, her tawny eyes gleaming gold with humor. "Now that the amenities are over, how about pouring me a cup," she suggested, leaning back comfortably to stretch out her long legs in front of her.

Kit observed her relaxed form with a jaundiced eye. "I'm barely up and you're practicing for the comic-of-the-year award." She took down another cup and filled it with coffee. "Do you want some toast, too?"

Summer shook her head while snagging a lightly browned triangle from Kit's plate. "I had breakfast ages ago. You forget we don't all sleep till noon."

"Or go to bed at dawn," Kit countered, taking a chair across from Summer. "What are you doing out by yourself? Don't tell me you left Brandon with the kids again?"

"No, I roped Gussie into watching them while I play hooky. Brand's off fishing with Joe on the *Sea Mist,* so I decided to visit you." She tipped her tousled head to study Kit. "You look different somehow—new makeup?"

Kit's fork, carrying a bite of delicately seasoned scrambled eggs paused halfway between her plate and her lips. "New makeup?" she echoed, bewildered at the abrupt question. "I'm not wearing any yet."

"Oh," Summer murmured, her gaze if anything more searching. "How's that girl—what's her name—Lydia doing?"

"Fine, as far as I know," Kit replied slowly before taking a taste of the perfectly prepared breakfast for which she no longer had an appetite. She had a sinking feeling her friend was much too perceptive or else she, Kit, had suddenly lost her ability to disguise her thoughts.

"Business?" One golden brow winged upward as Summer probed further.

"Never better." Kit placed her fork deliberately on the edge of her plate and eyed her persistent questioner. "Why are you here?" she asked, her tone warning Summer she would accept no evasions.

Summer stared back at her in silence for a moment before shrugging gracefully. "Would you believe I'm not sure? Maybe it was intuition? Or maybe it was the way you sounded last Sunday? Or perhaps it's because I haven't heard from you in days and that's not like you. Brandon swears when we visit, I spend at least half my time flittin' about with you," she added spreading her hands in an inadequate attempt to convey her meaning. "You know, if there's something wrong, I'd like to help."

Kit glanced down at her plate, touched by Summer's unreserved friendship. "Is it so obvious?" she murmured without raising her eyes. She laughed slightly, more in self-mockery than in humor. "I must be losing my touch."

"Or reaching out," Summer opined gently.

Kit lifted her chin, her eyes reflecting a protective

blankness. "Explain please." The command was softly spoken.

"Next to Brandon, you're the most private person I know. For all your social contacts, your crazy escapades and even the occasional strays you pick up, you remain above it all. Not aloof exactly, certainly never cold, but very detached." Her gaze swept the vividly decorative kitchen. "Do you know Sunday was the first time I've ever seen you confused or off-balance?" She held up her hand when Kit would have interrupted. "Don't give me that line about that kid's uncle. Not unless it's a great deal more personal than his bad opinion of you."

Kit hesitated, torn between confiding in her friend and playing dumb. Neither course really appealed, although for widely differing reasons. Her fingers traced an abstract pattern on the blue woven place mat. "How did you feel about Brandon in the beginning?" she asked finally, the words escaping without thought from her lips. She saw Summer's eyes widen at the unexpected query and wished she had guarded her tongue more carefully.

"Annoyed, to tell you the truth, and too damned attracted to him for my own good," Summer replied after only the slightest hesitation. "Kit, we're not eighteen-year-old girls—just what are you asking me?"

Kit shook her head, her eyes revealing her newly awakened love. "I suppose I'm trying to ask you what it feels like when you're in love," she admitted. Her voice lowered on the last word until it was scarcely above a whisper. "I never have been, you know. And now I find that I'm having my first love affair." She grimaced expressively. "Talk about late-starters."

"Tyler?" Summer questioned.

Kit nodded. "Black eyes, sexy body, disapproval, et cetera," she responded, all thoughts of her barely tasted breakfast long since forgotten. "And there's Ben standing between us. I feel like I'm betraying Ty by not telling him about them. Ben wants to be honest as I do, but Lydia's still afraid. And every time Tyler and I are together I feel worse. Half of me believes he'll understand and forgive us. But the other side remembers all too well how angry he was about Lydia in the beginning." Once started, Kit was amazed at how open she was being. With the simple act of telling Summer her problem, she felt somehow easier.

"What about him? What does he feel? Surely if he loves you he'll believe your motives were good, even if he's angered by the way you adhered to them?"

Kit stood up abruptly, prodded into action by the utterance of the very question for which she had no answer.

"You know as well as I do that a person can feel passion without love."

"True," Summer agreed, frowning at Kit's restless movements. "This really has got you tied up in knots, hasn't it?"

Kit glared at her from over her shoulder. "That's putting it mildly. One minute I'm up and the next I'm down. Emotional roller-coasting is definitely not my idea of the way I want to live my life."

Summer rose with feline suppleness. She stretched lazily, a tiny commiserating smile curving her lips.

"Well, honey, all I can say is welcome to the human race." She deftly collected their half-filled mugs of cold coffee and carried them to the sink.

Kit watched her clear the table, a flash of irritation in her eyes. "You could at least sound a little sympathetic," she pointed out.

Summer shook her head, her smile widening into a full-grown grin. "Not me, my friend. I've seen you in action too often. You'll deal with this."

Kit tried and failed to hold on to her annoyance in the face of Summer's cocky assurance. "Darn you," she muttered, her lips twisting into a reluctant smile. She moved to the sink and began filling it with water and detergent. "I'll bet you're just enjoying the idea of me struggling with my relationship like you did with Brandon. Misery loves company and all that."

Summer faced her accuser, her golden eyes glittering with wicked mischief. "Now that you mention it—" Her retort was interrupted by the ringing of the doorbell.

"Get that, will you?" Kit asked, her hands wet and soapy.

Kit started to wash her plate, her ear catching the murmur of a deep masculine voice mingling with Summer's slow drawl. Something about the rich cadence captured her attention, bringing her head up with a snap. Ty? What was he doing here, she wondered silently as she quickly dried her hands. She was almost to the kitchen door when Summer appeared on the threshold, a roguish glint in her eyes.

"Look what I found at the front door," she teased.

Kit's fleeting glance promised retribution when it

captured Summer's golden eyes. "Is something wrong?" she demanded, turning to Ty. Immediately she was conscious of everything about him, from the shower-damp lock of hair blown carelessly across his brow to his long, tapering legs encased in casual brown and gold plaid slacks.

"No, nothing's wrong," he answered, making a slow, comprehensive sweep of her scantily clad body. "Are those shorts or is it the bottom half of a bathing suit?"

"It's cutoffs," Summer supplied obligingly, noting Kit's bewilderment over his comment on her abbreviated attire. "Kit has a positive mania for wearing clothes a quarter of an inch away from microscopic."

Ty nodded, grinning with unabashed, lusty approval. "You'll have to admit she's very circumspect around the club."

Kit's eyes lit dangerously as her lover and her best friend exchanged understanding glances. How dare they discuss her as though she weren't even there? When did they get to be such good friends? Unreasoning jealousy rose in her throat at the thought. She glared at both of them, seething with reaction yet unable to say a word. Even in the midst of her anger, she knew her responses were way out of proportion. Mentally counting to twenty—a trick for regaining control that she hadn't had to use since she was a teenager—she fixed a smile on her lips.

She ignored the curiosity in Summer's eyes at her silence and the speculation in Ty's. "Don't you have somewhere you have to be?" she prompted in a voice that, miraculously, held only good-natured friendship.

"Yes, I guess I do," Summer agreed, her head tipped in pretended consideration. She turned to Ty with a wide, friendly smile. "Get Kit to bring you to our next barbecue. I know my husband, Brandon, would enjoy having you to even up the odds."

"Odds?" Ty repeated, obviously at a loss. He looked first at the tousled blonde in front of him, then at Kit, searching for enlightenment.

Kit found her humor taking an upswing at his perplexed expression. "I'll explain," she offered, chuckling. She waved Summer on her way. "You know where the door is, captain."

Barely aware of the other woman leaving, Ty stared at Kit, drinking in the sight of her. "I'm waiting for my explanation," he prompted, forcing the ordinary, irrelevant words out in an attempt to divert his mind. Suddenly all he could remember was Kit's silken body lying beneath his and the hungry moans she'd made as she arched against him. The need to hold her again, to feel her move in a passionate rhythm of his making was almost overwhelming.

"Women against men," Kit supplied briefly. She read the desire smoldering to life in Ty's eyes with delighted anticipation. For a gloriously free moment she forgot all of the reasons she shouldn't and remembered only that she had. "Don't look at me like that," she purred, closing the short distance between them with fluid, graceful strides.

Ty lifted his hands, curling them possessively around the exposed curves of her shoulders. "I can't help it," he admitted huskily, his ebony gaze flowing over her face to her throat and the champagne-silk valley between her breasts. "Was it only yesterday?" He raised his eyes to hers.

"An eon ago," she breathed in her own throaty admission.

"I promised myself I wouldn't do this. Yesterday was unplanned, but now . . ." His words trailed off as his fingers gently traced the subtle hollows of her feminine form.

Reality intruded, bringing Kit back to an unwelcome sanity. "I know." She sighed as she absorbed the warmth of his touch for a moment longer. Then, knowing she must, she stepped reluctantly away.

Ty let her go, his hands hovering for a moment in the air between them before he dropped them to his sides. "I came to take you to lunch with Emily," he announced, his eyes holding hers with an unwavering intensity.

Shocked at his statement, Kit stared at him. Was that a plea she saw? She wondered. "Why?" she asked bluntly, well aware that Emily had resisted every attempt she had ever made to meet her. Not that there had been many, she acknowledged fairly.

Ty opened his lips to speak as he glanced automatically at his watch. "Emily—" he began, then stopped abruptly. "Trust me enough to change for lunch and I'll explain everything on the way. We really don't have time now."

Kit searched his expression, aware of his need for her agreement. It was surprisingly easy to offer him the trust he asked for. "All right," she answered, seeing his tension dissipate with her words. "Just give me ten minutes."

10

Okay, we're on our way, so explain, please." Kit turned her body slightly so that her back was angled between the car door and seat back.

Ty threw her a wry glance, his lips twisting into a small grimace. "Sometimes I wish you weren't so direct."

Kit raised her brows at the muttered comment. "Well, you have to admit this invitation is unexpected. First Ben and now me. I never have been able to figure out why Emily had him over that Sunday."

Ty negotiated the midday traffic with practiced ease while focusing most of his attention on her. "Actually, I'm the one responsible for that. I have been trying to get Emily to meet you since I finally realized you weren't what we thought. I told her about your cousin and how he'd noticed Lydia and how the two of you had been keeping an eye on her." He frowned briefly, recalling Emily's continued stubbornness where Kit was concerned. "I thought if she realized that Mallory's was kind of a family operation, she might feel less threatened."

"It must have worked, because she did agree to see Ben," Kit pointed out, glad the riddle of Ben's invitation was finally solved.

"She only did that as a compromise," he retorted in partial answer, knowing she could fill in the blanks herself. Admittedly, it was a small effort to soften Emily's opinion. He couldn't bring himself to state his sister's animosity more clearly. Yet he knew he had to warn Kit about his sister's ongoing reluctance. In spite of the fact that Kit was well able to handle anything Emily dished out, he still wanted to protect her.

Kit half expected just this type of situation. From what Lydia had confided about her mother, Kit had drawn a fairly accurate picture of Emily's personality. Devoted wife and mother, she had given herself almost completely to her home and family. Devastated by her "loving" husband's desertion, she had channeled her energy into earning a living for herself and Lydia and into being a "supermom" to her daughter. And that's where the problems began. Lydia had balked at Emily's strictures and at the heavy demands made by her mother's job. Little disagreements grew into full-scale arguments between a bewildered and rebellious Lydia and her equally bewildered and frequently tired mother.

"Why now?" Kit asked, watching Ty carefully. "If she hasn't changed her mind, why this lunch?"

Having become accustomed to speaking his mind without self-censorship, Ty had no compunction about being totally honest. Kit deserved the whole picture without the soft-edged evasions he would have employed with another kind of woman. "Part of it is to accommodate me, since I'm the only family she's got besides Lydia." He paused just long enough for the implications of his answer to make themselves felt. "Plus I think she wants to meet the woman who seems to have succeeded where she thinks she's failed."

"Great," Kit mumbled dryly, wondering who deserved the most sympathy: Emily, for having the problems she obviously had; Ty, for having to give counsel in a situation where there were no right answers or cut-and-dried procedures; or herself, for being caught in the crossfire?

Ty eased into the crowded parking lot at their destination, switched off the engine, then turned to Kit. His face was an expressionless mask, his eyes dark and unreadable. "I don't need to tell you how much this meeting could mean to Lydia." Neither with gesture nor glance did he touch her—he didn't dare. Now was the wrong time and this was the wrong place. But nothing—no amount of will power—could suppress the emotions tugging at him. She was so calm, so peaceful; she was an oasis of tranquility for him in the midst of his family's crisis.

Kit read his emotional withdrawal and wondered at it. She wanted to touch him and reassure him that everything would be all right. She had always been able to recognize another's pain or worry, but now she actually felt his hurt and his concern. Loving him had given her this gift and responsibility.

"I know," she answered finally.

The simplicity of her softly spoken acknowledgment released the strange tension holding Ty motionless. He lifted his forefinger to stroke the gentle curve of her cheek. "I can't promise Emily won't be difficult," he warned, his eyes warm with all that he was feeling. He had tried to hold himself aloof and failed. But he felt no loss; rather, he had won. The depth of emotion he saw in Kit's face strengthened him in some curious way. She would make this work if it was humanly possible. He trusted her.

"We'd better go in," Kit suggested.

Ty sighed. "I guess so." The leather of the car seat rasped as he slid out of his side and came around to Kit's. He glanced down at her when she stood beside him on the walkway. "Will you remember my opinions aren't my sister's?"

"Yes," Kit murmured with a faint smile.

He was seemingly content with her brief reply. Touching his hand to the base of her spine, he guided her toward the entrance of the restaurant.

Fragrant hibiscus lined the boardwalk-style path winding beneath feathery palms. In spite of the importance of the coming hour, Kit was aware of the carefully landscaped beauty of one of her favorite seafood haunts.

"Have you been here before?" she asked as Ty pushed open the natural wood door, allowing a gentle waft of cool air to escape.

"Many times," Ty admitted. "I'm a seafood lover

and this place is one of the best in the area." He touched Kit's arm lightly, directing her attention to an alcove across the crowded dining room that overlooked the inlet. "Emily's here already."

Grateful for the noon rush keeping the hostess busy, Kit studied the woman she had come to meet. Deceptively casual blond hair, a shade lighter than Lydia's, complemented the tanned, Florida look of Emily Nelson. A soft, uncrushable dress of pale green complete with cool white accessories created an image that was businesslike as well as feminine. With her eyes trained on the spectacular water view, Emily appeared at home in these elegantly affluent surroundings.

It was only when the hostess stopped at her table and Emily realized they had arrived that Kit got the full measure of Lydia's mother. Blue eyes so like her daughter's held pain and barely controlled hostility, sweeping Kit from head to toe before settling on her brother's face.

"You're early," she murmured in an attractively modulated voice.

Ty frowned at his sibling, clearly displeased with Emily's greeting. "Emily," his tone was a warning and a reprimand, "this is Kit Mallory." He glanced at Kit, his gaze for her softer than his words. "Kit, this is my sister, Emily Nelson."

Emily's conventional reply was anything but sincere, Kit decided as she took the chair Ty courteously pulled out for her. Stifling the urge to respond with an equal amount of reluctance, Kit held on to her best public manner by remembering Lydia's needs, and Ty's.

Not that it did much good. Emily obviously had her own plans, beginning with probing questions into Kit's past and her present activities as a bar owner. The first Kit answered simply and briefly, having no desire to explain to her questioner the depth of her own teenage rebellion. It was enough that she knew why it happened and how it turned out. On the second issue she was more forthcoming. Unexpectedly, Kit found that here, the one area where she had been certain Emily would be the most disapproving, Emily actually showed a flicker of interest and, even more surprising, admiration.

"I can't believe you took on a renovation project of that magnitude when you were doing so well," Emily commented after finishing the last shrimp in her cocktail.

Kit smiled, understanding her disbelief. "It was a risk, considering the percentage of repeat customers and regulars I had. People don't always respond well to change," she agreed.

Emily glanced at her sharply, as though a hidden meaning lurked behind her words.

Kit saw the look, interpreted it and put on her most innocent expression. She was aware of Ty's alert scrutiny. Throughout the conversation he had kept his own participation minimal. He only stepped in when Emily appeared to forget herself and allowed sarcasm to creep into her tone.

"When Dan died so unexpectedly, I felt like my life had lost its rudder. We'd always been close, even more so after my mother passed away." Kit hesitated, wondering fleetingly why she suddenly felt the need to reach out in a personal way to this woman. Was it really only because she wanted to help Lydia and Ty? Or could it be because Emily's pain was so akin to what she knew her mother must have felt?

"And?" Emily prompted, her eyes brilliant with her need to know Kit's feelings.

Kit stared at her, forgetting Ty, where they were and everything that had made them reluctant companions. "I needed to prove myself both in a financial way and an emotional one. Dan was gone, he wasn't coming back. I was alone with no one but me to depend on."

"Were you scared?"

Kit nodded her head almost without conscious thought. "Not often, but yes, I was afraid. I'd have been a fool if I hadn't been." She grinned suddenly, her mood lightening with effort. "Neither my mother nor Dan raised me to be a fool." Sobering once again, Kit continued, "Anyway, I decided to make a plan for both myself and the business. I decided what I wanted and what was essential to my well being and my security. Once I had that, I had a direction." She spread her hands in a gesture of completion. "It worked."

Emily was silent, a thoughtful look on her face. Kit angled her head subtly until she could read Ty's expression. The faint smile lifting the corners of his lips held approval and gratitude. Warmed by his regard, Kit touched his hand slightly, covering her movement by lifting her glass of iced tea to her lips.

"You know, all I really considered when my husband left was how Lydia and I were going to live. It never occurred to me to look deeper," Emily explained slowly, her words emerging more as thought patterns than conversation. "Maybe I should have." She met Kit's eyes, her own noticeably less hostile. "I still don't think my daughter should be anywhere near your place."

The abrupt rider drew a swift reprimand from Ty. Kit stilled his next comment with a shake of her head.

"Neither do I," Kit replied.

Emily was as taken aback at her firm response as the silencing gesture Kit had made to her strong-minded brother. "You don't," she faltered, dividing her glance between the two of them. "Why?"

Kit shrugged. "For one thing, Lydia is still underage and will be for a while. And frankly, I value my business and my reputation too much to want the kind of trouble Lydia could bring," she stated bluntly. "And I care about Lydia herself. While she's much more settled and behaving with more maturity than she did three months ago, she needs stability in her life. The security of being loved and having a family. She won't get that in my bar."

Skepticism warred visibly with the lingering remnants of hostility in Emily's expression. "Ty's been telling me all along that I've been wrong about you," she offered hesitantly. "Until now I didn't believe him." She shifted her gaze to her brother's face, as though seeking his approval or, perhaps, his forgiveness.

The vulnerability of her expression wasn't lost on Kit. For the first time she understood the depth of Emily's antipathy toward her. Somewhere mixed up in the welter of Emily's emotions was the worry that she was losing her brother as well as her daughter to Kit's influence. Ty's pushing for this meeting could only have aggravated the situation. Kit wanted to reassure her, but was unable to think of a way to do it. As with Lydia, Emily had to find out on her own.

Emily refocused on Kit, the sleek image of an up-and-coming real estate agent replaced by a mother's concern. "I'd better be going. I'm supposed to meet Lydia at school to talk to her counselor." She rose, finding her handbag. For a moment she hesitated. "Thank you for coming," she whispered before turning swiftly and walking away without looking back.

"You did it." Ty's deep-throated statement conveyed the full range of his surprise. "I'd hoped she would listen, but I hadn't allowed myself to believe she would change her mind." He caught her hand, wrapping his fingers around her slender bones.

Kit returned the pressure, enjoying the warmth of his touch. "She hasn't altered her opinion completely," she reminded him, her lips curving into a gentle smile. The relief on his face, the gratitude in his eyes fed her hungry heart. She had given him a small gift of her love, if he only knew it. As for herself, perhaps her secret would soon be revealed. Then and only then would she be free of the pricks of conscience coloring her time with Ty.

"What are you thinking?" Tyler asked, watching her intently. "You looked worried for a second. I thought you'd be pleased."

His expression invited her confidence, unknowingly deepening the guilt Kit felt over her continued silence.

"I was thinking about all of us," she replied, producing the truth minus the subtleties behind it.

A light flared to life in the inky depths of Ty's eyes at her admission. "You and me—us?" he clarified swiftly, making no effort to disguise his interest.

Kit's lashes swept down in an involuntary attempt to shield herself from the need Ty had revealed. "No—yes," she halted, annoyed at her hesitant reply. She lifted her eyes to his, suddenly knowing she had to tell him. Right or wrong, she could not deceive him by omission any longer. "Ty, we need to talk," she began, her tone clear and determined.

"I know," he agreed at once. His gaze flickered significantly around the restaurant before returning to her face. "But not here and unfortunately not at your place or mine either," he added, grimacing as he checked his watch. "I've got a plane to catch in a little over an hour."

"A plane?" Kit echoed, puzzled.

Ty released her hand and tossed a couple of bills on the tray containing their lunch tab. "It's only going to be an overnight trip so I can take care of that account I told you about."

Kit rose, undecided whether she should be disappointed or glad her confession was being postponed. "I can call a cab to take me home," she offered, trying to match Ty's suddenly businesslike tone.

He shook his head. "Your place is on my way and you know it." He cupped her elbow, his fingers encircling her arm possessively. "Don't go all calm and polite on me now."

"What did you say?" Kit demanded when the door

of the restaurant closed, leaving them alone on the walkway leading to the parking lot. "I'm not the one who went from lo—friend," she substituted quickly, hoping he wouldn't notice her slip, "to businessman in the blink of an eye."

Ty frowned down at her, surprised at the irritation distorting her usually tranquil expression. "I know we need to talk, honey. You can't want it any more than I do." He paused, eyeing her strangely. "So much has happened in such a short time, surely you . . ." He spread his hands, indicating his frustration and inability to adequately express what he was feeling. "What I'm trying to say is, let's save this until I get back and we have the time we need without me rushing off to catch a flight."

Reasonable though his argument was, Kit had never been in a worse frame of mind to listen. But she knew she had to if she was to have any chance of making Tyler understand her position and the motives behind her actions.

"All right," she conceded with obvious reluctance. "But the moment you get back . . ." Her voice trailed away, leaving the urgency of her request to linger between them.

"Kit?" Ty questioned, concern clouding his eyes. He lifted a hand to grasp her chin when she averted her head. Silently he probed her closed expression, seeking a reason for her unusual behavior. "If it's this important to you—" he began slowly, only to be interrupted.

Kit shook her head, dislodging Ty's fingers. "No, you're right. We'll get together when you get back."

Kit heard the edge in her voice and inwardly winced at the brittle sound. Was that really her? Could she have been counting on telling him that much? "We'd better go," she said, starting down the path. If it was an effort to escape her disturbing thoughts, she hoped only she realized it.

Ty kept pace with her, occasionally glancing at her carefully composed profile. He didn't touch her; he sensed somehow that she needed the solitude of her own space. What was wrong? he wondered, suddenly recalling the faint glimpses of this same withdrawal in the past. She had been so honest, had given so freely of herself before, yet every once in a while she seemed to retreat. If he hadn't come to trust and respect her, he would almost categorize her behavior as being guilty.

Kit was aware of the assessing quality of Ty's silence as he drove her home, but she made no move to break it. After all, what could she say? I love you, Ty, but I've been lying to you from the moment I met you. I slept with you, knowing my twenty-two-year-old cousin was in love with your underage niece. I sanctioned the pairing in spite of knowing Ben was in no position to support a wife. Stark as they were, those were the unchangeable facts. There were so many other factors that dictated her behavior, but would Ty understand? Would he even give her the chance to explain?

"You wanted to see me, Kit?"

Kit glanced up from the bar order she had been trying to concentrate on with a frown. "Yes," she replied, gesturing to Ben to close the door. "I need to talk to you." There were those words again. They had haunted her all afternoon.

Ben sprawled into a chair, his brows raising in curiosity at her short temper.

Kit rotated the pencil she held, her eyes focused on the brilliant scarlet cylinder. "I met Emily today. She started out being hostile, but toward the end she seemed to soften." She lifted her eyes, focusing on Ben's expectant expression. "If there's ever going to be a time to tell her and her brother, I think it's now," she pointed out, openly stating what they both knew.

"Lydia is still holding back. I could go to them myself and explain," Ben offered slowly.

"No, it must come from Lydia. We both know that. Part of the problem all along has been her immature reactions to her situation. If she can't handle herself like an adult now, when will she be able to? You need a wife who's a woman, not a child. And Lydia needs to take responsibility for herself." Kit paused, giving her words time to sink in. "I think she can do it with your support."

"Believe it or not, I think she can too, but how do we convince her?"

"I've been thinking about it and I may have a solution." She ignored Ben's surprised relief and continued. "Why don't you and Lydia stop by at about eleven tomorrow? I'll explain then." Kit could read the questions in Ben's mind, but she ignored them. Her plan was vague at best and she needed the night alone to think it over.

And with Ty out of town, that was what she had.

Sleep eluded her as she tried to consider all the possible alternatives. So much depended on how Lydia and Ben explained themselves. Ben and Lydia's relationship, Lydia and her mother's rapport, or what there was left of it, and of course, attraction between Ty and herself. The wrong approach could irreparably damage them all. As for Tyler—Kit forced her mind away from what might lie in store for them.

Their desire was strong and rich with fiery passion. On her side there was love to strengthen the white-hot need she had for him. But Ty? As far as she knew, he had only respect and a small measure of trust to offer her beyond the sharing of his body. Without love, could those tentative feelings withstand the knowledge she had hidden from him?

11

The morning sun flickered faintly through an enveloping mist. The unusual fog was created by the cool night air mating with the warm temperature of the earth and the nearby sea. Kit stood at her window, watching the gradual lightening of the damp, gray world outside. Stretching muscles cramped from a restless night that had ended with her in a chair in front of the window waiting for the dawn, she sighed. Shadow lifted his head at the weary sound.

"It's been a long night, my friend," she said, stroking his sleek head. "And it's going to be an even longer day." She rose slowly, the lithe lines of her body unfolding with natural grace beneath the wispy emerald nightgown she wore. Her hair cascaded down her back in a riot of red gold curls. The chestnut shade appeared even richer in the faint light from the window.

Padding soundlessly on bare feet through the apartment, Kit let Shadow out for his morning run. Today she had neither the desire nor the energy to join him. She made coffee, then showered and dressed automatically. Like the world outside, she seemed enshrouded in a clinging gray cloud. Yet, unlike her counterpart in nature, hers would not burn off with the rising of the sun. But there would be an end to the limbo of waiting. Keeping that thought in mind, Kit completed her household chores before preparing a light, if belated, breakfast. She had just finished drying the dishes she had used when the doorbell rang. Ben and Lydia had arrived.

Kit silently led the way to the living room. She sat down, facing the pair occupying her sofa. Her first look at Lydia's face when she'd opened the door had warned her that this interview would be anything but easy.

"Did Ben tell you why I wanted you both to stop by?" Kit asked quietly, giving the upcoming discussion a starting point. She spoke directly to Lydia, her steady gaze holding the younger girl's emotion-filled one. Defiance, pain and anxiety looked back at her from the troubled blue depths, reminding Kit very much of their first meeting. Something had happened to upset Lydia.

"Oh, he told me all right," Lydia replied with a surprising amount of adult bitterness in her voice. "You've thrown in with Mom and Uncle Ty, I hear, so I guess I should've expected this."

"'Thrown in'?" Kit queried calmly. "You have a basis for that remark?"

Ben shifted uneasily. "Emily told Lydia—"

"I asked Lydia," Kit interrupted firmly, her eyes never wavering from Lydia's tense face.

"Well, it's true, isn't it?" Lydia burst out. "I know you all had lunch together yesterday and I can guess who you were discussing. First you, Mom and Uncle Ty and then that stupid counselor at school are all trying to run my life." Agitatedly, she jumped to her feet. "I know what I want. Why won't any of you listen to me? I love Ben. I know I'm young. I know I have no training. But I can get it." She glared at Kit, the pain-filled words stopping as abruptly as they'd begun. Her breasts heaved beneath her thin cotton pullover top. "Why did you do it, Kit?" she whispered miserably. "I trusted you. I thought you were my friend."

Kit rose and closed the space between them. "I am, Lydia. I always have been and I always will be. I didn't betray you," Kit offered slowly but with sincerity.

Lydia searched her quietly composed features, a faint hope flickering in her eyes. "You didn't?"

Kit shook her head. "No, I didn't." She hesitated, choosing her words carefully. "I think you're also wrong about your mother and Ty, too. They're no more your enemies than I am."

Lydia stared at her pityingly. "They took you in," she observed with sadness. "My mother and Uncle Ty, between them, intend to send me to Auburn University when I graduate. Mom has a friend up there who's pulling some strings to get me in since my grades are so borderline."

"When did you find this out?" Ben demanded, looking as shocked as Kit felt.

Lydia flung herself back on the couch. "Yesterday," she admitted. "I don't want to go. She knows I don't want to go, but she won't listen. She just made all the arrangements without telling me a thing about it."

"Damn," Ben muttered, glancing at Kit in frustration.

"I'll run away and get a job until we can be married," Lydia suggested wildly, a reckless tilt to her chin. "I'll be eighteen soon, so they won't even be able to make me go back."

"No!"

"No!" Kit's voice blended with Ben's in a unanimous decision.

"You don't want that, honey. You know you don't," Ben pointed out with gentle reasonableness.

Lydia's eyes filled with tears of frustration and defeat. "I know, I know," she breathed tearily, moving into Ben's waiting arms. She buried her head in his shoulder, sniffing despondently.

Ben cradled her protectively, looking as upset as the girl he held so tenderly.

Kit turned away from them, feeling she was intruding. She walked into the hall to give them some time alone. A flicker of movement in the long, decorative, glass insert to the right of her front door caught her eye. Not wanting whoever it was to ring the doorbell, she quickly released the lock and opened the panel.

Her eyes widened at the sight of Ty standing before her. "Oh, damn," she swore beneath her breath, her disbelieving gaze sweeping him from head to foot.

He grimaced, obviously having heard her involuntary oath. "I had hoped for a better reception," he observed with an odd lack of emphasis. "I've been working flat out ever since I left you just so I could get back here." The husky timbre of his voice was deeper than usual and laced with weariness.

Kit traced the new, clearly etched lines marking his features, well able to believe he had done just that.

"May I come in?" he prompted when she made no effort to invite him inside.

Kit cast a swift glance over her shoulder, wishing her apartment had suddenly changed its interior design. There was no way she could let Ty in without him seeing Ben and Lydia together. But what could she do? She couldn't send him away—it would look too suspicious. Reluctantly, she stepped back.

"I'm sorry. I'm not exactly functioning well at the moment," she apologized. She laid her hand on his arm as he stopped beside her, waiting for her to close the door. "I have someone here." She moistened her lips carefully, her eyes pleading with him to listen. "It's Lydia. I—"

The rest of her explanation was smothered by Ty's satisfied murmur. A second later, she was left staring at empty space as Ty turned on his heel and headed for her living room. Recovering swiftly, Kit hurried after him, nearly bumping into him when he stopped short just over the threshold. Kit bit her lip to keep from groaning aloud at seeing Ben and Lydia in what appeared to be a passionate embrace.

"Lydia!" Ty roared, anger darkening his expression

and tensing his body. "What the devil is going on here?"

At the knife-edged ejaculation of her name, Lydia jerked guiltily out of Ben's arms. "Uncle—Ty," she stammered, her cheeks flushing under his thunderous regard.

Ty swung around, including Kit in a searing look.

A shiver touched Kit's spine at the cold emotion in the ebony depths. Whatever chance she had ever had to make him understand was gone. By his eyes' own evidence, she had been convicted. Her lashes swept down to hide the intense hurt slowly filling every cell of her body. No blessed numbness of shock for her. No, only an agony beyond simple pain.

"Why don't we sit down?" she suggested so calmly even she was surprised by her level tone. In spite of everything, she had to see this situation through. Forcing herself to ignore her own feelings for the moment, she returned to her chair.

Somehow her small prosaic action signaled the end of the utter stillness that had fallen when she'd spoken.

"This isn't what it looks like," Ben got out, surging to his feet. He faced Ty, ignoring or unconcerned with Ty's physical advantage of size and finances.

"Don't, Ben," Lydia pleaded, jumping up at almost the same instant. She glared at her uncle. "I'm an adult," she snapped. "You have no right to treat me like some overeager schoolgirl."

Ty took a step toward the pair, his hands clenched at his sides until the knuckles showed white. "Don't talk to me about schoolgirls. Why the hell aren't you in class? And what are you doing necking with a twenty-two-year-old kid?'' he demanded, incensed.

''Necking?'' Lydia parroted scornfully, drawing her petite frame up to its full height. ''I was not necking, as you call it!'' she shot back angrily. ''I was kissing the man I'm going to marry!''

Silence. Utter, complete silence followed Lydia's fiery announcement. Forgotten, Kit stared at the frozen scene. Unguarded emotions flared in each of the faces. Ty's was angry, disbelieving. Ben's was concerned, protective, strengthened with a hint of pride and satisfaction. And Lydia—hers was a revelation. The weary, defeated expression she had worn only seconds before was gone. In its place the clear-eyed determination of a woman fighting for her man had arisen. The change sat strangely on her youthful, untried features, but it was in no way diminished by the contrast.

''You can't marry without parental consent,'' Ty pointed out in a deceptively mild tone that fooled no one.

''Believe me, I know,'' Lydia returned immediately. She tucked her hand in Ben's. ''Even if I could marry Ben right now I wouldn't. I'd be nothing but a burden to him. I have no training and until he finishes school he hasn't the money to support us both while I learn a skill.''

''I love Lydia,'' Ben added quietly, his control clearly showing his maturity. ''But she's right.'' He glanced down at the golden head lightly brushing his shoulder. ''I want her for my wife. This second, if I could, but it's just not possible.''

Ty studied them without speaking, his brow furrowed by a deep frown. He jammed his hands in his pockets and took the last unoccupied seat in the room. His eyes flickered briefly over Kit's still figure before returning to the younger pair.

"As Kit said, why don't we sit down," he drawled. He waited until Ben and Lydia complied with his suggestion before continuing. "Now, suppose one of you starts from the beginning and explains how Lydia went from a teenage rebel to an undeclared fiancée in the short period of three months. And while you're at it, I'd also like to know why no one bothered to tell either Emily or me about any of this."

"There was never—" Ben began immediately, only to be interrupted by Lydia.

"Let me, darling," she said with so much composure that Ben and Ty stared at her in surprise.

Not so Kit. Having no real place in the scene being enacted in her living room, she had observed Lydia's sudden realization of her own maturity. In spite of the pain she felt at the confrontation with Ty that loomed in her future, Kit couldn't help but be glad Lydia was showing the strength Kit had always known she had.

Lydia faced her uncle bravely, her clear blue eyes steady. "You know all the things that drove me away, so I won't repeat them. But I will admit my behavior has been downright stupid." She hesitated. "Or at least it has been some of the time. Anyway, I stumbled onto Mallory's because some of the kids at school had been raving about it and trying to figure out a way to get in. They didn't make it, but I did."

She grimaced, a flicker of pain shadowing her face

for a moment. "I really intended to get roaring drunk that first night. But I couldn't." She turned to eye her love with a knowing look. "Somehow my drinks tasted more like ginger ale and juice than liquor." She caught the guilty look Ben tried to hide. "So I was right." She nodded, clearly unsurprised, before refocusing her attention on her uncle.

"The fourth night I went there I got one drink before Kit showed up at my table. God, I was scared. All the kids at school knew how hard she is to fool. But my ID was good and I got by on that. I didn't get by on being an unescorted female. I had to either have a date or stop coming." She shuddered, remembering how terrible she had felt at being politely asked to leave. She stared down at Kit's sapphire carpet as she gathered herself for the most difficult part.

"Somehow I started talking. I couldn't seem to help myself. Something about Kit and the way she just sat there waiting made me want to tell her everything." She raised her head and looked straight into Kit's eyes. "You never said I was stupid, silly or childish. Not once through all my tantrums. I needed you and you were there."

Lydia's poignant words created a pool of silence, each face mirroring the effect of her confession. Kit saw each expression clearly and shared the emotions reflected. Pain, love, need and loneliness. "Go on," she prompted softly, wanting—needing—an end to this recital. For herself and for them all.

"It felt so good to have someone listen, someone who didn't judge. I begged Kit to let me come back. She did, on the condition I didn't drink and that Ben

173

would keep an eye on me." She shrugged, her hands fluttering in a faint gesture of nervousness. "We got to know each other. We went out when he had time. We fell in love. I know now I should have told Ben I was only seventeen. But I didn't. I was too afraid he'd send me away. I couldn't have stood that." Tears gathered in her eyes. "He's forgiven me for lying, Uncle Ty. Can't you at least understand, if you can't forgive me too?"

Ty studied his niece without speaking, his black eyes searching the young face and the hauntingly adult emotions it conveyed. This was no fit of rebellion, he acknowledged. He heard the strength in her voice and recognized the need she made no effort to disguise. He switched his gaze to the man at Lydia's side. Ben's arm curved protectively around Lydia's shoulders even as he stared back at him. He had liked Ben when he met him and if Lydia had been of age, or even through with her schooling, he would have been pleased to think of them together.

"What if I don't agree to this?" he asked curiously, with an intensity that fooled no one.

"We never asked you to agree to anything," Ben pointed out carefully, but without sarcasm. "It would be better for Lydia if you and her mother could be happy for us. Lydia wants to finish school and I still have a year left myself before we can even think about marrying. But if neither of you is prepared to support Lydia while we wait, I will. And I don't just mean financially," he added, just in case Ty got the wrong idea.

Ty's lips curved faintly at the edge in Ben's voice. "I never thought you did," he soothed.

"I want to take some bookkeeping courses when I graduate. Math has always been one of my best subjects. With that kind of training, I can get a good job almost immediately and start getting stuff together for when we do get married," Lydia interposed eagerly. "Help us, Uncle Ty. Help me convince Mom I'm not pulling some crazy stunt like I used to just to get attention. Help me show her I can act responsibly."

Ty glanced at Kit. "You agree with this?"

"I do," Kit stated firmly, knowing that by giving her support, she might be relinquishing any chance she had with Ty. The urge to plead her own case had never been so strong, yet she couldn't. Either Ty trusted her or he didn't. She stared into his black velvet eyes, keeping her own as tranquil as possible. It took every bit of self-discipline she possessed to control her clamoring emotions.

"I'll speak to Emily for you." He turned to face the pair on the couch. "I can't promise I can make it easier, but I'll do my best not to make it any worse."

"Really?" Lydia breathed, silent tears of relief tracing silver paths down her cheeks. At his nod, she buried her face in Ben's shoulder.

Ben gathered her in his arms, staring at Ty over Lydia's golden head. "You won't regret helping us, I promise you. I might not be what you would have wished for Lydia, but I do love her and I will take care of her. Just as she'll take care of me."

Kit watched the man-to-man exchange with her own sense of relief. Ben and Lydia would make it. Ben had the drive and now that Lydia had grown up enough to begin planning and handling her life, she would make him a good wife and partner. Each had something to give the other. Her gaze followed Ben as he shepherded Lydia out of her living room to take her home. Finally she and Ty were alone. Now it was their turn.

Slowly, she brought her eyes back to Ty's face to find him studying her with a curiously intent expression. There was no hint of softness in either his features or the unblinking ebony depths probing her being. He was so still he could have been carved from stone. Then he spoke, his voice a harsh sound torn from the depths of his soul. "Can you ever forgive me, Kit? I seem to have been constantly judging you and I've never been right once."

Whatever Kit had expected, it hadn't been Ty's agonized self-condemnation. "I don't understand," she whispered, hardly daring to hope this wasn't the end for them. "I lied to you."

"So you did," he agreed with a gesture of dismissal. "But you had no choice." He rose and came to kneel before her. "In your place I'd have done the same."

Astonished at his humble position at her feet, Kit sat frozen in her chair. They were on eye level with each other, separated by a few soft breaths of air. "You're not angry?" she asked, longing to reach out to him, yet afraid to.

"For a moment, when I first came in, I was," he admitted huskily. "Then I saw your face and I knew

176

your pain." He lifted his hands slowly, as though wary of frightening her. His palms cradled her face, his fingers splaying lightly from her temples to the base of her throat.

"How could I have ever thought your eyes were calm. They're not, you know," he murmured huskily. "Right now they're filled with questions, a little hope and so much caution."

Kit dropped her lashes, shielding the mirrors of the soul he read too easily. What was he saying?

"I love you, Kit Mallory," he rasped, brushing her cool lips with the warmth of his own. "Trust me. Open your eyes and tell me you love me too. I won't hurt you again, I promise."

"When did you know?" Kit whispered, still hiding in the safetly of her blind world. Her fingers curled around the upholstered arms of her chair as she inhaled the rich male scent of him.

"I knew I loved you when I got back to Jacksonville and discovered I was lonely. I was up to my ears in work and yet I was so lonely for the sound and feel of you I could hardly concentrate." His lips coaxed hers with gentle, teasing kisses. "Please, Kit, look at me."

Slowly, unable to deny the depth of feeling she heard in his rich voice, Kit opened her eyes to stare directly into his. Fathomless pools of night, dark with secrets and filled with mystery. Yet even in deepest midnight the stars still shine. Ty's love blazed forth to light the darkness with the intensity of the brightest astral body.

"You really do love me?"

12

Come let me show you how much." He took
her hands in his. His warmth flowed into her limbs
as he pulled her to her feet. "Come with me to my
place."

Kit followed the pressure and the guidance of his
hands for two steps, then halted. "Not there," she
refused, making a decision.

Ty's face contorted at her refusal. "Kit, I—" he
began.

Kit silenced him with a shake of her head. "Here,"
she whispered softly, finally giving free rein to the love
she had held prisoner for so long.

Ty searched her expression. "You do love me," he
growled triumphantly, sweeping her into his arms and
striding toward her sunlit bedroom.

Kit felt the shudder that went through him when she

twined her arms around his neck and heard his broken sigh of relief against her hair. He had been as unsure as she. The realization went through her like cognac, heady, powerful, with a fire spreading through her in expanding waves. She moved her head slightly until her lips touched the pulse beating so strongly at the base of his throat. With a low moan, she opened her lips, tasting the heat and sweetness of his skin.

"God, woman," Ty groaned, releasing her so that she slowly slid down the long length of his body. Feminine thighs, hips, breasts flowed over him, increasing the desire burning within him. It was a subtle torture so agonizingly sweet he savored it to the last aching touch.

Kit inhaled, making an incoherent sound. Her slim hands moved beneath his dark, casual shirt, tugging upward impatiently, hungry for the feel of his naked skin beneath her palms. "Help me," she demanded, her voice a hoarse plea.

Ty shrugged out of his shirt with a graceful, muscular twist so that he was bare from the waist up. His body gleamed gold in the sunlight filtering through the bedroom windows. His skin rippled with each movement. His face was drawn by need and anticipation as he bent his head to capture Kit's mouth.

Her blouse and bra vanished beneath his fingers while his tongue stroked her. When his hands cupped her breasts, Kit's body melted into liquid waves of pleasure gathering, building, with each caress. She arched against him, her muscles tight with the desire only he could create and assuage within her. The rest of their clothes disappeared, somehow burned away

179

by the fire consuming them. A moment later Kit felt the undulating cushion of her water bed against her back.

Ty pinned her beneath him with one strong leg thrown across hers. With a hoarse groan deep in his throat, he tore his mouth from hers. Before Kit could protest she felt his tongue wrap around the pebble-hard crest of her breast. His teeth nipped gently on the rosy bud before it was taken into the heated dampness of his mouth and consumed with a thoroughness that pierced her loins with white-hot shafts of fire.

She twisted under him, barely able to breathe for wanting him. Her fingers raked from his shoulders to the curved contours of his hips, seeking to know him, his strength, his passion and his love. When her hands slipped between their bodies to find the source of his desire, his body tightened like a bow drawn to its fullest measure.

For an instant he thrust against her caress, eyes closed, his face finely etched with the emotional force driving him. He touched her soft skin with an urgency that was rough yet exquisitely gentle. His mouth roamed hungrily over her, devouring the secrets of her body, claiming the intimate essence of her with a passionate caress that brought waves of pleasure surging through her to crest and break in an ecstasy of indescribable delight and fulfillment.

"Body, soul and mind. You're my woman, Kit," he vowed. He slipped swiftly up her body, one powerful hand stroking the length of her. He pulled the long braid of her hair across her throat, using the end as a feathery duster for her breasts. He held her motionless while he pleasured her with the erotic patterns he drew on her quivering body. "Marry me, my love," he demanded, a primitive smile echoing the hot look in his eyes. "Come live with me and love with me."

The desire raged so strong in Kit she had no words to give this man. Wanting, needing to offer him the gift of her desire as he had given to her, she reached for him. Her hands kneaded his body, savoring him with her palms and fingertips and gently raking her nails over his golden skin. Yet her caresses were inadequate. She had to have more, she had to have all of him.

"Let me love you," she breathed against his taut abdomen. She lifted her eyes to read the surprise, the hunger he made no effort to conceal. She saw her answer in the black-velvet depths.

She flexed her fingers like a sensuous feline, rubbing her hands over his stomach and thighs. Teasing him, she avoided his most sensitive flesh while at the same time caressing him with her hands and the damp whisper of her tongue. She glanced up to find him watching her every move, a look almost of wonder on his face. She smiled, unaware of how desirable she appeared with the thick braid brushing across her naked breast, her lips swollen red from his possession and her body shimmering with the pleasure she wanted to share with him.

With a small moan, she leaned down to gently explore the final territory that was hers. Her lips moved over his warm skin and the dark hair that had the texture of raw silk. She savored him, fascinated by his maleness, his strength and his virility. He was all that she wanted, all that she needed to fill her being and her life.

When her tongue traced his length, she felt his body tense beneath her in anticipation. He arched toward her, revealing without words his delight in her. Desire burned within her at the power and vulnerability of the passion they shared. With a soft sigh, she let the world slip away as she loved him as she had loved no other before him.

"Kit."

Her name echoed as he thrust upward toward the fulfillment only she could provide. She eluded his hands, intent only in stoking his fire with the pleasure of her body. She held him for a few moments, much too involved to realize he'd caught her at last.

The world tilted crazily and suddenly she was staring into his eyes as he lifted himself over her. "Ty." His name was a demand and a plea.

"Mine," he muttered thickly, his hands closing over her breasts possessively. "I've never known a woman to equal you."

Kit arched her hips, digging her nails into his shoulders. Sweet as his words were, she wanted more. She cried out when, with a deep male growl, he joined them as one. He filled her completely, setting an ancient rhythm of barely leashed savagery that goaded her to match him. His tongue filled her mouth, fusing his breath with hers as he pushed them ever closer to the summit of desire. Suddenly, borne on a searing thermal current, they were there. She drank his hoarse cry, feeling his powerful body quiver as he filled her with the very essence of himself. He gave to her and she gave to him. Two made one.

"You never did say yes," Ty's voice rumbled softly in Kit's ear when his breathing returned to normal. He gently shifted his weight to one side.

Kit caught him close, reluctant to be separated from him. She smiled, tightening her body to hold him cradled in her warmth. "You need to ask?" she teased with a smugly satisfied expression.

Ty framed her face with his hands, his eyes searching hers. "Yes. I need to hear you say it. I'm through jumping to conclusions about you."

"Yes," she whispered throatily, fitting herself more closely against him. If she had needed an affirmation of the change in Ty, she had it now. Whatever differences still lay between them no longer mattered. Together they could do anything as long as they loved and trusted each other.

Taking advantage of the lull in the many good wishes coming her way, Kit retreated to a softly lit corner of the room. All around her clusters of friends, both old and new, laughed and talked, enjoying the holiday atmosphere of Mallory's II. Even Summer and Brandon had flown down early from Boston just to be there. Bright Christmas streamers, golden bells and strategically placed bunches of holly reflected the Christmas season as well as proclaiming the grand opening of her new business.

Kit's gaze roamed over the lounge, lingering briefly on the small group of smiling people across from her.

Ty's surprise had been the high point of the evening she decided, watching Ben, Lydia and Emily behaving as the family they were soon to be.

"Happy, honey?"

At the sound of Ty's voice, Kit turned her head, a smile curving her lips. "Yes," she replied simply. She relaxed against his hard body as he wrapped his arms around her waist. Her long braid, interwoven with gold, red and green ribbons, was trapped between them as Ty fitted her snuggly against his length.

"Ben and Lydia look good together, don't they?" Ty murmured, his breath feathery against her temple.

Kit nodded, glancing toward the trio once more. "Emily seems to be enjoying herself too. I'll confess I was surprised to see her here."

Ty's embrace tightened briefly at the faint undertone of pain caused by Emily's persistent disapproval of Ben and Lydia's relationship even after their marriage. "She asked if she could come. She's finally understood what happened and your part in it."

Ty sighed, well aware of how hard the last year had been on Kit. In spite of his support, his sister had reverted to outright hostility and anger when she found out about Lydia and Ben. All the progress Kit and he had made had been virtually wiped out by her attitude. Yet oddly, Lydia had matured almost overnight. She had held on to her determination to marry Ben until finally even Emily was convinced. She and Ben had become officially engaged at the end of the summer, with the wedding date set for the following February.

"I never thought Emily would come around," Kit murmured, following Ty's thoughts with uncanny accuracy.

Ty caressed her ear with tender lips, having no desire to discuss his troublesome relatives. "Tonight's a celebration, remember?" he whispered huskily.

"I know," Kit purred softly, brushing her head against his chest in a feline gesture of pleasure. "I still don't understand why you wanted the opening to be held on our anniversary."

Ty's black eyes darkened with gravity and tenderness at her vaguely plaintive tone. It was far from the first time his love had asked this question. "It's my anniversary present to you."

Startled at the seriousness in his deep voice, Kit turned in his arms to face him. "I thought these were my gift," she replied, lightly touching the delicately fashioned diamond teardrop earrings she wore.

Ty shook his head, his gaze holding hers. "That was only one of them." He traced with his eyes the clear curves of her features and the love that shone in her sherry-colored eyes. He lifted a hand to cup her chin.

"You gave up so much to move to Jacksonville with me, your friends, your home and your business." He covered her lips with a forefinger when she would have spoken. "I know Ben's a good manager and I know one day he'll make a fine partner, but it's not the same. When you came to me, you had to start all over again. You've slaved over getting this place ready, yet you still had time to give to me. I wanted you to know how much I admire and respect what you've accomplished here. And more importantly, I wanted you to know you have my support in whatever you do," he finished on a deep note of sincerity.

Kit stared into the ebony-velvet eyes. Where once only disapproval and reluctant desire had burned, now love and commitment glowed as bright as the sun. He was the mate she'd never thought to find, the love she'd never expected to know. He filled her nights with passion and her days with strength and peace. But most of all he loved her.

"I love you, Harrison Tyler," she vowed, lifting her lips for his kiss.

Ty lowered his head until his mouth hovered a mere breath away from hers. "You're the woman I've waited for all my life without even knowing it. You're strong, you're capable, a fitting partner for any man. But you're mine, as I'm yours. I'll never leave you." Then his lips claimed hers with a hunger he made no effort to hide. A hunger that had consumed him from the first and had increased with every moment he shared with his woman—his wife—his love.

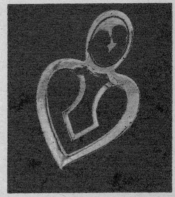

READERS' COMMENTS ON SILHOUETTE ROMANCES:

"I would like to congratulate you on the most wonderful books I've had the pleasure of reading. They are a tremendous joy to those of us who have yet to meet the man of our dreams. From reading your books I quite truly believe that he will some-day appear before me like a prince!"

— L.L.*, Hollandale, MS

"Your books are great, wholesome fiction, always with an upbeat, happy ending. Thank you."

— M.D., Massena, NY

"My boyfriend always teases me about Silhouette Books. He asks me, how's my love life and natu-rally I say terrific, but I tell him that there is always room for a little more romance from Sil-houette."

— F.N., Ontario, Canada

"I would like to sincerely express my gratitude to you and your staff for bringing the pleasure of your publications to my attention. Your books are well written, mature and very contemporary."

— D.D., Staten Island, NY

*names available on request